'In order to have the heir that I wish for, I obviously need a wife too,' Fabian said. 'What I am proposing, Laura, is that you enter into a strictly business arrangement with me to achieve both those ends. In return, you will lead a comfortable, prosperous life as the mistress of the Villa de Rosa and the mother of my child.'

It was as though a cyclone had swept through the room and left her stunned and dazed. It had appeared out of nowhere, without warning... After such a shocking visit, the room, and *her*, would never be the same again. In contrast, Fabian radiated extreme calm—the absolute antithesis of her own wild tumult.

'I can hardly take it in... Are you being serious?'

The plastic wallet of papers slid out of her grip and onto her lap. She grabbed it just in time, before it fell onto the floor.

'Do you think I am making a joke?' He scowled. 'I know my proposition may come as something of a surprise, even a shock...but trust me. I do not come to such decisions lightly, or without giving them the proper consideration and thought.'

'But if you are in earnest ab̶o̶u̶t̶ ̶s̶u̶c̶h̶ ̶a̶ ̶p̶r̶o̶p̶o̶s̶a̶l̶ why pick *me*?'

The day **Maggie Cox** saw the film version of *Wuthering Heights,* with a beautiful Merle Oberon and a very handsome Laurence Olivier, was the day she became hooked on romance. From that day onwards she spent a lot of time dreaming up her own romances, secretly hoping that one day she might become published and get paid for doing what she loves most! Now that her dream is being realised, she wakes up every morning and counts her blessings. She is married to a gorgeous man, and is the mother of two wonderful sons. Her two other great passions in life—besides her family and reading/writing—are music and films.

SECRETARY MISTRESS, CONVENIENT WIFE

BY
MAGGIE COX

MILLS & BOON
Pure reading pleasure

First published in Great Britain 2008
Harlequin Mills & Boon Limited,
Eton House, 18-24 Paradise Road, Richmond, Surrey TW9 1SR

© Maggie Cox 2008

ISBN: 978 0 263 86461 8

Set in Times Roman 10¾ on 13¼ pt
01-0908-40899

Printed and bound in Spain
by Litografia Rosés, S.A., Barcelona

SECRETARY MISTRESS, CONVENIENT WIFE

To everyone at the Miracle Café
for the inspiration I receive every time I go there!

CHAPTER ONE

'*Mio Dio!*'

Jet-lagged and irritable, Fabian Moritzzoni pressed his fingers between his brows and sighed heavily. Finally, in complete exasperation, he rose up from his seat. Outside, the sound of passionately raised voices sliced through the atmosphere—an ill-timed bombardment he was unprepared for and could well have done without. And the loudest voice of all belonged to his housekeeper, Maria.

By the time Fabian reached the twin front doors of his palatial home, the tail-lights of a battered silver Fiat were careening away at speed down the wide, gravelled drive, and Maria stood glaring after them, her hands planted firmly on her amply fleshed hips as though she was quite prepared to take on the whole Roman army if she had to.

'Are we being invaded?' Fabian demanded in his native Italian. 'Because that's what it sounds like!'

'The nerve of these people! The audacity! Who do they think they are?' Turning her affronted gaze towards her employer, Maria passionately elaborated, 'They were from the press, Signor Moritzzoni. I caught them sneaking around, taking pictures of the villa. Then, when I confronted them, they demanded an interview with you about the anniversary concert and about the celebrities that are going to be there. I sent them packing with a flea in their ear, I can tell you!'

'They should be speaking to Carmela if they want an interview. No doubt she has organised something to that effect already.'

Shaking his head from side to side, Fabian sighed. Then, in spite of his irritable mood, he found himself succumbing to the wryest of grins.

'I am fortunate indeed to have you around to protect my privacy, Maria. It is better than having a personal guard! But do me a favour, eh? Keep the volume down first thing in the morning…respect for my poor head, yes?'

'Of course, Signor Moritzzoni. Shall I make your coffee now and bring it to you?'

'That would be very good. Thank you.'

Taking his espresso coffee with him, Fabian followed the long, winding concrete path down to the elegant orangerie at the end of his lush private garden. Sitting down beside an intricately fashioned wrought-iron table outside on the terrace, he glanced back towards the graceful Palladian house that dazzled in the early-morning Tuscan sunshine, and at the plethora of pristine white marquees that had been erected in front of it. At the end of the coming week those marquees would be milling with the cream of Italian glitterati, as well as family and friends, all attending the now famous concert that Fabian organised every year in memory of Roberto Moritzzoni— his father.

The house was, inevitably, a hive of activity, in preparation for the big event. Add to that the altercation outside earlier with the press, and he craved some time alone to drink his coffee and think his thoughts in peace. Although the notion of peace and his father definitely did *not* go hand in hand…

The prospect of the coming concert had been playing on Fabian's mind for days now, and had induced the tension and irritation in him that he'd come to know only too well. Add to that a frightening schedule, travelling here there and everywhere, and he had to own to not receiving the same satisfaction and pleasure from his work as he normally did. As a highly successful businessman, dealing in valuable art as well as giving support to several important and worthy charities, his presence seemed to be in almost constant demand, and lately he had had the compelling notion that he ought to jump ship for a while and really look at where his life was going. God knew, a review was well overdue.

Scraping his hand through the strands of his dark gold hair, he grimaced. With such a gruelling work schedule a restorative vacation seemed light years away, never mind the possibility of the other pressing item that had been on his mind of late—*marriage and children*.

'So this is where you are hiding. Maria said that she'd seen you head this way.'

Her pretty mouth shaped into a teasing grin, his PA, Carmela, suddenly hove into view. He'd been so preoccupied with his thoughts that Fabian hadn't even registered her approach. Inevitably accompanied by her trusty notepad and pen, she was clearly primed and ready for work. *So much for time on his own to sit in quiet contemplation!*

'I have been back but one day in my own house, after my trip to America, and it is like returning to a football stadium! Apart from my private suite, I swear there is not one room anywhere that is not overflowing with people! Do you wonder that I have to hide?' Fabian grumbled.

Carmela gave him another broad grin. 'Poor Fabian! But I have some good news for you, so perhaps hearing it will cheer you up.'

'And what is this good news you have to cheer

me? You are not going on honeymoon just before the concert after all?'

Carmela's grin disappeared. 'Of *course* I am going on honeymoon, Fabian! I have already postponed it once in deference to the demands of work. Vincente is a patient man, but not *that* patient! No…I came to tell you that my friend Laura will be arriving from the UK later on this afternoon, and I will be showing her the ropes so that she can take over from me when I leave the day after tomorrow.'

'Stepping into your shoes and handling such an important event is a big responsibility to put on the shoulders of a novice, Carmela. Are you sure this friend of yours will be up to the task?'

'She's been a music teacher for some years now, and has also organised some local concerts where she lives, so she's not exactly inexperienced. And she will, of course, be very familiar with the artistic aspect of the work.'

'Does she speak Italian?' Pressing his fingers against the tender spot between his dark gold brows again, Fabian winced, as though some medieval instrument of torture was doing its best to bring him to his knees.

'She's a very fast learner, and when I was at school with her in London she was always top of the class in languages. Anyway, your own English is practically perfect, so you won't have to worry.'

'Good…just as long as she does not expect me

to hold her hand and guide her every step! Quite frankly, I will be very glad when this whole tedious affair is over and my home can return to normal.'

Tossing back her head of raven curls, Carmela took instant umbrage. 'The concert is a wonderful event that raises a lot of money for the children's hospice. Surely you do not regard the privilege of holding it as "tedious", Fabian?'

'Of course not! That is not what I meant at all!' Now it was *his* turn to display offence. 'Okay,' he continued impatiently, 'let us get back to your friend. I am very grateful that you have found her for us. Has she been to Tuscany before?'

'No. I have invited her many times, but in the past few years things have been rather difficult for her, and circumstances did not allow her to make the trip. She tells me she is definitely overdue for some sunshine, and I know she will fall in love with this place and the beautiful Villa de Rosa…who could *not*? That reminds me… I must speak with Maria to check if Laura's rooms are ready. That is the other positive aspect of the situation that should help make things less stressful for you, Fabian. She'll be here on the premises whenever you need her. Shall I get you another coffee? That one looks as though it is going cold.'

'Please.' Pushing the cup in its matching cream saucer towards Carmela, Fabian could no longer suffer in silence. 'And bring me a glass of water and something for a headache, will you?'

'Perhaps you shouldn't have any more coffee if you have a headache?'

'So you are my mother now, as well as my assistant?'

'I was only trying to—'

'You should know by now I am *impossible* without my coffee in the morning! But take heart, Carmela... In a day or two you won't have to think of my needs. It will be your very fortunate husband who will command *all* your attention!'

Yet again her boss's wry humour prevented her from feeling too indignant, and his young assistant immediately forgave him his grouchy mood. She realised he had a lot on his plate, and that he was probably handling it a lot better than most would do in his situation.

'I will bring what you ask and make sure you are not disturbed for an hour at least...will that help?'

'If you can do that you are a miracle-worker!'

'A moment ago I was your mother!'

Rolling her eyes heavenwards, Carmela hurried away, and as he watched her retreat Fabian found himself considering yet again the rather intricate subject of a wife and heir. Intricate because he was not at present in a relationship, nor intended to be. When a man had been scorched by flame once in his life he got wise to the danger, and learned never to stand so close to the fire again. But he was thirty-seven years old, and time was not standing still.

Because of his considerable wealth, and the responsibilities that came with the ownership of the palatial Villa de Rosa—the home that had been in his family for centuries—he needed a son or daughter to inherit. No…there simply had to be another way to get what he wanted other than embarking on some doomed love affair. Over the next few days he would seriously apply himself to finding the solution.

'It's so good to have you here at last! It's been such a long time…*too* long! Of course I am looking forward to my honeymoon, but it would be so nice to be able to spend some time with you. Promise me you won't run off straight away when I return in two weeks' time?'

Regarding the perfectly groomed, curvaceous brunette who had been her best friend at school, Laura wondered how the intervening years since they'd last met had flown by so quickly. It had been at least ten years since they'd seen each other. Of course they'd kept in regular contact by letter and e-mail, and sometimes by phone, but it wasn't the same as seeing someone on a regular basis and having the chance to deepen your friendship with them. But now that she was here in Tuscany Laura was determined to make the best of the opportunity that had fortuitously come her way.

Carmela's offer of a job—albeit a temporary one—had been a Godsend, quite frankly. Laura didn't even mind that this was to be no holiday, because music was her absolute passion. Just to be around it would do wonders for her spirit and morale, she was certain.

'I don't have a job to return to as yet, Carmela,' she answered now. 'So I have nothing to rush back to the UK for.'

'That is good to hear. Not that you don't have a job, of course, but that you will be able to stay and visit me properly!'

'I've been looking forward to renewing our friendship for a long time.'

Laura crossed her arms over the pretty white antique lawn and lace blouse she wore with a pastel blue skirt, and her smile was genuinely heartfelt. Then, with a soft sigh, she turned her grey eyes away for a moment, drawn by the beautiful sunlit gardens she saw through the huge Palladian windows.

The white roofs of the elegant marquees glinting in the afternoon sunshine reminded her of a medieval joust, where richly dressed lords and ladies would make their entrance at any moment to take their seats for the coming performance. The sea of white made a stunning contrast against the surrounding shimmering green of the perfectly mown lawns. In the distance was an ornate white marble balustrade, with steps just beyond it leading into what was clearly a much more private section of the garden. Meanwhile, the scents of honeysuckle and wisteria drifted through the opened windows, filling the air with a soporific fusion of rare delight. *It was like stepping into a dream...*

'And what do you think of your rooms?' the dark-haired girl pressed eagerly. 'I've put you near the back of the house, where it is a bit more private should Fabian have guests staying, and the views from your windows are quite spectacular!'

'They're lovely, Carmela—just lovely! I shall be able to indulge every girl's fantasy of being a princess with such elegant rooms to myself, as well as sleeping in that beautiful four-poster bed!'

'Carmela—have you spoken to the press yet? This morning they— Excuse me. I did not realise that you had company.'

At the sound of that richly voiced Italian, Laura turned. Viewing the man that was responsible for it, she saw him momentarily hesitate, his glance sweeping over her with mild surprise, before entering the room. There was a strange kind of tension immobilising her, that made her thought-processes feel as if someone had pressed a slow motion button. *Was this Carmela's boss?* If it was, he was the antithesis of what she'd been expecting.

Golden-haired, blue-eyed, with a strong, lean jaw and of an imposing height, he might easily have hailed from Denmark, Sweden or even Germany. Yet the confident, slightly arrogant way he bore himself, and the way he wore his clothes—as though they and he were in complete enviable accord—easily convinced her he was a true son of Italy.

Azure, they called the colour that was so reminiscent of the Mediterranean, and that was the startling hue conveyed by this man's disturbingly direct glance as he focused it on Laura. Feeling heat assail her from all sides, she quickly looked away—taken aback that she should experience such an emphatic reaction to someone she'd only just met.

'Fabian! You're just in time to meet Laura. She arrived only an hour ago, and I was just about to come and find you to introduce you.' Putting her hand behind the fair-haired girl's back, Carmela impelled her forward, as if concerned she would be too reticent. 'Laura, this is Signor Fabian Moritzzoni... owner of the Villa de Rosa and my employer. Fabian, this is my dear friend Laura Greenwood.'

Automatically Laura held out her hand, and felt the man's large cool palm enclose hers, his clasp neither too firm nor too slack, yet without a doubt signifying authority—and she found herself immediately under disquieting surveillance.

'My pleasure, Signorina Greenwood. It appears I

am indebted to you for agreeing to stand in as my assistant in Carmela's absence. You had a good journey from the UK, I trust?'

'I did, thank you.'

'And this is your first time in Tuscany, I hear?'

'It is, but that's not because of any lack of desire. Carmela's been asking me to visit for ages, but somehow it never seemed to be the right time. Still…I'm here now and I hope that I'll be able to be a real help to you, Signor Moritzzoni.'

'That is my wish too, Signorina Greenwood.' Fabian's tanned brow furrowed slightly as he gazed back at Laura. 'So. You will take the rest of the day off to settle in, and presumably start work tomorrow? Carmela will put you in the picture about what needs to be done. Does that meet with your approval?'

His unsettling examination didn't waver for an instant. He had the glance and acuity of focus of the shrewdest of businessmen. Laura would not like to be on the receiving end should she be someone who was trying to deceive him. But then she thought of something else. Had he seen the scar? Was that what he was looking at so intently? She lifted her hand automatically to touch the pale golden strands of her fringe, suddenly self-conscious of the disfigurement beneath it. No doubt it must displease him, in this land of the terrifyingly good-looking to gaze upon a woman whose already average looks were marred by an ugly scar. She wished he would finish talking to Carmela and go. Her confidence and determination in taking this job and making a success of it had not disappeared—but it had definitely been a little shaken.

'There's no need for me to wait until tomorrow to make a start,' she said. 'If Carmela needs me to give a hand straight away, then that's fine with me. I want her to be able to leave for her honeymoon with a settled mind, knowing that she's left the situation in good hands. The sooner I get to grips with what needs to be done, the better.'

'You see, Fabian?' Carmela cheerfully exclaimed. 'I told you there would be nothing to worry about with Laura here!'

'I am sure that you are right.'

His voice was smooth as amontillado and oloroso sherry combined—nonetheless, Laura detected a definite edge to the Italian's disturbing glance that seemed to say *I will be extremely disappointed if you should let me down.* Inwardly she shivered as her eyes determinedly met his, and it took every ounce of will she possessed to hold his gaze and not look away.

CHAPTER TWO

SINCE the arrival of the opera company and the orchestra that morning for rehearsals the house and grounds had joyfully vibrated with the sound of music and song. Listening in wonderment, Laura wished the children she'd taught could hear what she was hearing now. They might only have been six or seven years old, but they'd quite quickly acquired a fine appreciation of some of the classical pieces that she'd brought into class for them to listen to, as well as enjoying listening to their teacher occasionally playing the piano. They'd all been so eager to learn an instrument too, and Laura had done much to encourage their fledgling interest. *But she hadn't taught her class for over two years now, and as a consequence there was a hollow ache inside her that couldn't easily be filled.*

There had been a time in the past when she'd dreamt of a career performing music herself, but once she'd discovered her love of teaching it to children she had honestly believed she'd found her true calling. Now, after a period of enforced rest and recuperation because of her accident, she would have to start the search for a similar fulfilling post all over again. As soon as she got back from Tuscany she fully intended to redouble her efforts to that end, but at the moment she was pretty much in seventh heaven here, in this stunningly exquisite house, helping out a friend in need. Her spirits and morale were already uplifted by the sound of the music around her.

While Carmela consulted her master plan for the concert, in order to properly explain it all to Laura and make sure she hadn't left anything important out, her friend busied herself with more practical things. She didn't want to be idle with so much clearly to be done. Everyone she met seemed to have a hundred and one jobs to do. That being the case, Laura took it upon herself to help out wherever she saw she might be needed.

On checking back with Carmela a while later, she found her still fine-tuning arrangements, as well as making some important phone calls that only she could deal with. Seeing that the kitchen staff were run off their feet, she gave them a hand by carrying trays of drinks and food to the hard grafting workmen on the site, erecting the stage and lighting inside the largest marquee.

'*Buongiorno*, Signorina Greenwood.'

Halfway across the lawn, transporting empty glasses back to the kitchen, Laura came to a standstill at Fabian Moritzzoni's greeting.

'*Buongiorno,*' she replied, aware that her voice was not quite steady.

The man had ruffled her, suddenly confronting her like that when she hadn't been expecting it. He was wearing a white linen shirt over ecru-coloured chinos, with his sunglasses pushed back on top of his darkly golden head, and his appearance had a raffish sort of Bohemian quality about it, rather than the look of almost intimidating businessman of yesterday—though it would be a foolish individual indeed who believed he was anything less than one hundred per cent sharp...one hundred per cent on the money in every way. Being so painfully aware of the charismatic quality of this man could potentially be the most distracting drawback to this job, Laura concluded. Immediately she recognised the indefinable threat he represented to her peace of mind, and the still tender, wounded part of her wanted to instantly retreat.

'I see that you are already in the thick of things. An event like this is a lot of work, no?' He smiled, utilising that gesture with the easy confidence of a man who had had the world's attention from the moment he was placed into his doting mother's arms as a baby. Next to the supreme vitality he radiated, Laura felt like a very pale shadow in comparison.

Fabian had forgotten how delicate-looking this replacement assistant for Carmela was. Yesterday he'd had an impression of snow-pale skin and enormous grey eyes in an elfin face, and today her fragility was further emphasised by the sight of a body as slender as the stem of a birch tree at the mercy of strong winds. Her white muslin top and slim fitting skirt could not help but draw his attention to her tiny waist, boyish hips and small breasts, and her fine blonde fringe did its best to conceal a painful-looking scar.

Fabian sensed his smile quickly turn into a frown. 'Where are you taking that?' he demanded, jerking his head towards the tray she carried. 'To the kitchen? Let me take it for you. It looks heavy.'

But as he reached for it Laura moved deftly to the side, her pale cheeks suddenly flooded with pink. 'I'm stronger than I look, Signor Moritzzoni!' she announced with spirit, and Fabian silently acknowledged feeling surprised at her vehement response. 'Presumably you're not going to pay me for letting someone else do the work?' she went on. 'Anyway…I don't want to hold you up. I'd best get on.'

When she would have moved away, Fabian had the oddest notion to keep her there for a moment.

'You are not holding me up, and I did not mean to cause offence by offering my help. However, I *am* surprised to see you doing domestic work when I naturally expected Carmela to be occupying you with the organisation of the concert.'

She blushed even pinker than before. 'I was just trying to make myself useful while she did some last-minute checking of the plan before showing me the ropes. I'd best take this to the kitchen and get back there, to see if she's ready for me now.'

'Signorina Greenwood?'

'Yes?'

'Do not forget that at midday we all stop for siesta…no matter how busy we are! The sun is far too hot to work then.'

'Thank you for the reminder,' she replied diffidently, before hurrying away from him.

'*Piccolo fiocco di neve*…little snowflake.' Giving quiet voice to the whimsical observation that had crept into his mind, Fabian broodingly watched her as she negotiated her way gracefully across the shimmering sunlit lawns towards the house.

Taking a further moment to remind himself of where he had been heading and why, he realised her appearance had drawn his attention as emphatically as an elegant hovering butterfly ensnared the gaze in an unexpected moment of quiet, contemplative delight.

* * *

At her friend's behest at the end of the day's work, Laura accompanied Carmela to the *piazza* in the village to have dinner with her and her husband in one of the bustling atmospheric restaurants there. Eager to experience some of the vivid flavours of Tuscan cuisine, as well as to meet Vincente, she was only too pleased to join them. Carmela's husband was as charming as she'd guessed he would be, with smouldering good-looks and an engaging sense of humour, and she took to him immediately.

Afterwards, while the newlyweds lingered over their coffee—their eyes clearly only for each other—Laura made her way from the covered eating area of the restaurant into the balmy *piazza* itself. Leaning against a wide stone wall, with her light stole loosely around her shoulders over her pale lemon summer dress, she observed with interest the parade of beautifully attired men and women who strolled casually by. This, she'd learned, was the *passeggiata*—a nightly event that took place in many towns and villages all across Italy. It was an opportunity for both sexes to openly admire each other and cast a glance over someone special who had caught their eye. Italians worshipped beauty in all its forms, Carmela had told her friend, and welcomed every chance to display and celebrate it.

Feeling pleasantly tired after her exertions of the

day at the Villa de Rosa, Laura experienced no guilt at taking a few moments out simply to enjoy the warm magnolia-scented evening and to join the rest of the onlookers in the *piazza*. There were some stunning-looking individuals populating the square, but none in her opinion that could hold a candle to the frighteningly attractive Fabian Moritzzoni. Surprised at such an out-of-the-blue and *definitely* disturbing thought, Laura felt a little flutter of unease in the pit of her stomach.

'*Buonasera, signorina.*'

A young man with flashing dark eyes and a dazzlingly white shirt passing by with a friend stopped deliberately in front of her and smiled. Taken aback at his interest, Laura knew the same debilitating sense of panic that she always experienced whenever a man glanced her way. Her scar made her extra-sensitive over her looks, despite her determination to try and ignore it. But she was definitely the odd one out in this outwardly harmless parade of beauty, and she'd best not forget it.

Briefly dipping her head in acknowledgement of the unknown man, and starting to withdraw, she was suddenly aware of something of a commotion not far from where she stood. Laura's gaze, along with that of the young men beside her, turned towards the tall, broad-shouldered owner of tarnished gold hair, who seemed to be heading their way. His progress was being impeded by several enthusiastic compatriots, eager to shake his hand and acknowledge him. It struck her then that Fabian Moritzzoni must be an important man in this community. His handsome face was wearing a patient smile as he returned the effusive greetings that came his way, and he seemed to command the equivalent adulation of a much admired celebrity, but for some inexplicable reason Laura sensed that all was not well beneath the smile that appeared so natural and sincere. *Was it the concert that was troubling him?*

Finally, he arrived in front of her.

'Signorina Greenwood.'

His glance made a desert of her mouth with its piercing directness. For a moment all thoughts were suspended as she bathed in that captivating sea of Mediterranean blue. After a deferential *'buona-sera'*, her uninvited companions politely made themselves scarce.

'Hello,' she breathed.

'I knew it was you. Your bright hair and equally bright dress singled you out. What have you done with Carmela and Vincente?'

'They're still at the restaurant, enjoying their coffee.'

'But of course… They are newlyweds and, I suppose, anxious to be alone together. I regret that my poor assistant has had to wait so long for the privilege. My schedule is clearly too insane if it has come to this and she cannot take leave even to go away on honeymoon!'

'Can you not do something about it?' Laura enquired.

'What do you mean?' His gaze narrowed.

'Well…sometimes it's good to have a review of things, don't you think? Might it not be possible for you to lessen some of your commitments and perhaps think about making your schedule a little less demanding?'

Fabian was still mulling over her surprising response when a gentle breeze lifted the edges of her fringe. Immediately her hand went up to pat it down again, and a shadow seemed to move across eyes the hue and colour of palest moonlight.

'I think I'd better go…' She tugged the edges of her stole closer together across the bodice of her lovely yellow dress, her smile uncertain and defensive. 'Carmela might be looking for me.'

Aware that she was obviously self-conscious about the scar marring her otherwise perfectly unblemished skin, Fabian wondered how she had acquired it. Then he told himself not to be concerned. She was only working for him, and other than affecting her ability to do the job she'd been hired for her personal business was just that…*personal*.

'If she was going to give you a lift back to the villa, why not let me take you?' he heard himself suggest. 'I am going back there myself shortly. We will go and find her and tell her.'

'I don't want to impose.'

'Nonsense! How could you possibly be imposing when you are working for me as well as sleeping under my roof?'

'In that case then I accept your offer...*grazie*.'

The night was inky dark, and roads like treacherous narrow ribbons were illuminated by the car headlights as Fabian smoothly confronted each one as if he regularly negotiated far trickier terrain—in even poorer light and with equal impressive ease. *His hands were fascinating to watch.* Lean, yet powerful, with flawless tanned skin—they would draw a woman's eye whether he were sculpting clay, digging in the earth or holding a child...

Laura cut off the thought abruptly, even though the picture it conjured up was almost too tantalising for words.

'Am I driving too fast for you?'

Both amusement and mockery wove through his compelling voice, and Laura glanced at his smiling profile with no little agitation. 'I have no doubt that you are perfectly in control, Signor Moritzzoni, but I'd be a liar if I told you that the minuscule width of these roads plus the speed we are travelling at *didn't* scare me! Would you mind slowing down just a little?'

The impressive Maserati responded to the lightest
touch from Fabian—like something wild suddenly
tamed—and immediately Laura sensed the powerful
machine slow down to a much more acceptable
pace. Her relieved sigh was clearly audible in the intimate confines of the luxurious interior, and a swift
glance from Fabian told her that he was still somewhat entertained by her caution. He probably thought
she was a complete scaredy cat. She had every
reason to be cautious, but her new employer did not
know that…

'Is that better?'

'Much… Thank you.'

'So what did you think of our little town, hmm?'

'I thought it was quite delightful. I got the feeling
that there was a real sense of community amongst the
inhabitants that's very appealing to a city girl like
me! The *passeggiata* was fascinating too!'

'We are a very traditional culture, as you probably
know, and that is more often reflected in the smaller
towns and villages. But Italy is also very modern…
more so in places like Milan or Rome.'

'They always seem such impossibly glamorous
destinations, hearing about them back in England!
And although I would definitely like to visit them, I
think I might just prefer your small town…even
though it might not be so modern.'

'So you are a traditionalist? The type of woman

who would prefer home and family to a career and a glamorous social life?'

'A glamorous social life has certainly never been on my personal agenda, but the conflict between bearing children and having a career doesn't seem to get any easier for most women. However, I do think that the decision to have a child is such a momentous one that the child's needs and welfare should *definitely* come before the demands of a career—you only get one chance at a childhood. But in an equal partnership that could equally apply to a man making that decision. If that view makes me a traditionalist, then I suppose I must be!'

For a few moments Fabian didn't reply. Withdrawing his gaze only very briefly from the winding road, he examined Laura's impassioned expression in the semi-dark, wearing a seriously thoughtful one of his own. 'It is good to know that there are still young women who care so deeply about the welfare of children that choosing to stay home to take care of them over pursuing a career is not seen as such a sacrifice,' he commented. 'When what values we have left in western culture have been so cheapened by television and the media it is reassuring to learn that not *everyone* is so enamoured of or fooled by them.'

As if by mutual agreement they fell silent after that—as though both of them were privately surprised that they had found some unexpected common ground—and it seemed almost no time had passed before they were travelling the final road to their destination.

'See?' Fabian said softly, his eyes crinkling at the corners with a suggestion of pleasure. 'There are the lights of the villa up ahead. We are almost home.'

Home... Laura wished her dream of what that entailed could be a reality...the reality her heart sorely longed for.

'Fabian has asked us to join him for lunch,' Carmela announced absent-mindedly as she breezed into the office midway through the morning. She picked up the master plan for the concert from her desk and glanced down at it with a small frown between her perfectly arched brows.

'He has?' On her knees in the middle of the sumptuously carpeted floor, unpacking yet another box of champagne flutes and checking that none was broken, Laura glanced up in shock and surprise.

The heat had descended like a tropical blanket, and the fans dotted round the room were rendered practically useless against such deadening temperatures. Her sleeveless pink linen dress clung stickily to her too-warm skin, yet Carmela looked as fresh and cool as an exotic water lily in comparison.

'I know I was meant to be leaving at midday, but

he insisted I stay for lunch and I agreed.' Glancing up from her clipboard, the Italian girl rested her lovely gaze on Laura. 'When Fabian insists on anything, one cannot really argue! Besides…he *has* been very good to me, and I do not like to disappoint him. He is a considerate, generous man…not a tyrant like some bosses you hear of!'

'Yes, but why would he invite me too?' Her brows drawn together in genuine puzzlement, Laura brushed a drifting strand of pale hair away from her face. 'I'm only here temporarily, and there's so much to do I really should just crack on. I can eat something later.'

'That will not do at all!' Carmela was aghast. 'I told you. Fabian was most insistent that we *both* join him. He likes to entertain when he is at home— which is not very often because he travels so much. It helps him unwind, and a lunch like this is also an opportunity for him to get to know you a little before you start to work together, Laura.'

'Well…in that case I suppose I should go.'

Summoning a smile, Laura silently reflected on the challenge of being driven home by her new employer last night—and now contemplating eating lunch with him today! The intimate arrangement of the seating inside his luxurious sedan, with its attendant and somehow sexy smells of leather and burnished wood, had made her far too aware of the man sitting beside her. So much so that every molecule of air around him had throbbed with the sheer force of his presence, and made it impossible for Laura to feel completely at ease. The conversation they had shared had worked its magic on her too. And even though Fabian had initially been driving too fast for her comfort, it had been a long time since she had felt so safe on a car journey.

The recollection of all this left a far too vivid impression on her already overloaded senses which was hard to dispel. But it was perfectly true what she'd said to Carmela. There was still so much to do, what with the concert scheduled to take place in just four days' time, and as confident as the Italian girl appeared to be in Laura's abilities, she had yet to *earn* that confidence.

Allowing himself the faintest of private smiles as he glanced round the elegantly laid luncheon table, Fabian started to relax. Surrounded by three very beautiful women, he had no argument about not being in his element.

As Aurelia Visconti—a vivacious raven-haired opera star from Verona—chatted to Carmela about her upcoming Caribbean honeymoon, Fabian found his gaze settling on the young Englishwoman. She looked a little flushed from the heat as they sat beneath the luxurious awning outside the orangerie, where they were dining, and her fine blonde hair kept descending in gentle drifts of diaphanous silk around her heart-shaped face…

He realised he was staring. 'You are a little uncomfortable with our climate, I think, Signorina Greenwood?' he commented, watching her pale eyes widen, as though she were startled from a dream.

Her fingers moved a little restlessly over the white linen tablecloth. 'I'll get used to it. Believe it or not, it was almost as hot in the UK before I left! Climates are changing all over the world, I think.'

'That certainly seems to be the case.'

'Still…when you look at the history of the world, the earth always seems to right itself again somehow. I don't mean to say we can't take steps to improve things, or admit our part in it, but at the end of the day it's out of our hands, isn't it?'

'Another indication, perhaps, that we are *not* the ones in charge?'

'Yes.'

'Not an entirely comfortable thought for those who like to map out their lives down to the finest detail,' he remarked with droll humour, leaning back a little in his chair. 'So…you are *not* one of those people, Signorina Greenwood—if you believe that our fate is pretty much out of our hands?'

'No. These days I neither plan nor look too far ahead. Life has a nasty habit of intervening whenever I try to control anything, I find.'

A cloud seemed to pass before her eyes, and Fabian intuited that her mind had visited a dark place for a moment. She was thoughtful and quiet, and seemingly without guile—it struck him how different she was from most women he got into conversation with. For a start there was not the slightest hint of flirtation in her eyes and—without being conceited—he had become accustomed to such an occurrence. Was she in a relationship and perhaps completely devoted to her partner? So much so that she would not dream of making eyes at someone else?

Finding the very concept much too alien to easily embrace, Fabian drummed his fingers on the table. He realised that he would not exactly be averse to Laura flirting a little with him. It was definitely time to divert his thoughts away from such dangerous ground.

'Carmela tells me that you taught music in England? What ages were your pupils?'

'Six and seven.'

'So young!'

'You are never too young to enjoy music.'

'And clearly, by the look on your face, you enjoyed teaching the subject to them?'

'I loved it, as a matter of fact.' Her blush was in evidence again, and Fabian couldn't help but derive pleasure from the sight of it. 'That's why I was pretty devastated when I lost my job,' she admitted.

'What happened?'

'I was in an accident.' Appearing as though she'd inadvertently taken a road she would clearly prefer not to go down, Laura grimaced. 'Consequently I had to take a long period of time off, recuperating. When it was time for me to go back, the school principal told me that the authorities had decided to close down the music department due to lack of funding, and therefore there was no longer a position for me. Music wasn't exactly a high priority in the school curriculum, but knowing how much the kids loved my classes, I think it's a crying shame that they took that view.'

Remembering how passionate she'd sounded on the drive home last night when talking about children, Fabian felt an undeniable tug of profound interest.

'Some educational establishments can be very short-sighted where the arts are concerned...but perhaps that will change in time, with enthusiastic teachers like you to point out the benefits?' he suggested.

'It would be nice to think so.'

About to enquire further about her work experience, and curious about the accident that had robbed her of her job, Fabian found his attention suddenly claimed by Aurelia Visconti.

Laying a smoothly plump hand bedecked with diamond rings possessively over his, her ruby-red lips forming a definite pout, 'Darling!' she exclaimed dramatically. 'You are making me feel quite left out, talking to your little English friend over there instead of me! I am sure she has plenty to do, helping to arrange the concert, without monopolising your valuable free time as well!'

CHAPTER THREE

LAURA didn't understand everything the other woman said, but she'd been listening to language tapes and devouring phrase books ever since she'd agreed with Carmela that she would fly out to Tuscany and act as her stand-in. Consequently she was quite capable of getting the gist of what the opera star's meaning was, even if the look of disdain in her eyes didn't render the message loud and clear.

All of a sudden she fervently wished that the final course would arrive. Then she could make her excuses and get back to work. In fact, she wondered if their host would protest if she bypassed the dessert altogether and left now? As she found herself glancing towards Fabian, and the possessive diva by his side, his startling blue gaze met and claimed hers for a long, perturbing moment. Her stomach dived into empty space, as though she were plunging off the edge of the earth.

'Is something the matter, Laura?' he asked, completely confounding her by using her first name and not the more formal address she'd been becoming used to.

'No…nothing's the matter. I was just wondering if you would mind if I didn't have dessert and went back to work instead? I'm anxious to keep on top of things and I—'

'It is my express wish that you stay until the *end* of our lunch!' Looking surprised, then furious, Fabian glowered formidably. 'I am not accustomed to my guests suddenly getting up to leave in the middle of a meal! As important as your duties undoubtedly are, they will just have to wait.'

Feeling everyone else's gaze on her now, as well as their host's, Laura knew the heat in her face must cover every shade from puce to cerise in one fell swoop. All she had wanted to do was escape a situation where she was struggling to feel at ease, and she genuinely wanted to get on with the job she'd been hired for. But instead she'd unwittingly offended the very man she couldn't afford to offend. His attention had returned to the dazzling creature by his side, but Fabian's hard, slightly arrogant jaw clearly confirmed her conclusion. Feeling miserable now, as well as hot, Laura reached for her glass of water and took a long draught of the ice-cold liquid, hoping it would help cool her embarrassment as well as quench her thirst.

* * *

Laura had been wished an affectionate farewell by a flushed and happy Carmela, eager to be off on her honeymoon at last, and had spent the rest of the afternoon familiarising herself with her new duties. She'd rung several of the companies that were providing their services on the night of the concert to introduce herself, and sent out a last small batch of invitations to staff at a local hospital. Carmela had deliberately kept a few back for this express purpose.

In the middle of arranging for flowers to be delivered from Fabian to the formidable Aurelia Visconti, at the villa she was staying at until just after the concert, Laura glanced up in surprise as the man himself put his head round the door. Could it be that there was something going on between him and the beautiful opera star? She told herself it was only human to speculate after the way the older woman had so clearly staked her claim on him for most of their lunch—although Carmela had mentioned in passing that her boss was divorced and unattached.

'How are you getting on with everything?' he asked.

'Fine so far.'

'No problems?'

Breaking off her telephone conversation, with her concentrated gaze Laura conveyed the fact that he had her full attention.

'Nothing I couldn't handle.'

'Good. I just came to tell you that I am going out

for a while, and do not expect to be back until later
this evening.'

'Okay.'

'And tomorrow you will be moving into my
office with me.'

'Oh…is that really necessary? I mean, I've just got
used to where everything is, and won't a move take
up valuable time away from organising the concert?'

'It will take up hardly any time at all. You will need
me around to ask questions, and sometimes to talk to
people and problem-solve. It will be easier for us both
for purposes of work if we are in closer proximity. Was
there anything you needed to ask me before I go?'

'Not that I can think of right now.'

Feeling heat throb through her at the realisation
that from tomorrow onwards she would be working
in the same office as Fabian, Laura willed herself not
to appear flustered by the news. The incident at lunch
had made her even more wary of the man than she'd
been initially, and she wished she could just erase it
from her memory. Yet, perversely, she'd also experienced frustration at not having a chance to ask him
more about the concert.

Their little exchange about life and planning had
prompted her curiosity about how he personally
viewed such things. Was the anniversary concert
something that was set in stone as far as Fabian and
his family were concerned? Did he ever find the re-

sponsibility of hosting such an event year in, year out, somewhat daunting—onerous, even?

Still she grappled with the idea of sharing an office with him...

'Then have a good evening, and enjoy the dinner that Maria is preparing for you,' he said now, the faintest suggestion of a smile touching his lips. 'My housekeeper is an exceptional cook, and she makes the best lasagne in Italy! *Ciao*!'

'*Ciao*...'

The next moment he was gone, leaving just a faint impression of sandalwood and spice hovering in the air, and the slam of another door outside somewhere indicated he was on his way out to his car. Was he visiting Aurelia at her villa, perhaps?

Impatient that such an irrelevant consideration should hijack her thoughts, Laura leant back in her chair behind a desk that screamed to be tidied and ran the flat of her palm over her hair. Shaking the soft fall of golden butter-coloured strands loose from its confining band, she sighed at the release of tension that flowed out of her neck and shoulders, as if a small trapped inlet that had been shut off by a boulder could now flow freely.

The delicious lasagne eaten, and most of the other staff and work teams who had inhabited the building and grounds all day now gone—along with the orchestra and the opera company—Laura found the huge gracious house had become blissfully quiet again. But, although relative silence prevailed, inside Laura's head all she could hear were echoes of the amazing music that her ears had been treated to throughout the day. She realised that despite everything she was feeling happier than she'd been in ages. She'd made contact at last with a friend she'd very much missed, and had been given this marvellous opportunity to work in an environment that was about as idyllic as she could imagine. Surely it was a sign that life in general was improving vastly?

Humming to herself, she inserted the final invitation to an after-concert supper party into its gilt-edged envelope—this was an event that Fabian was throwing for some local dignitaries—and put it with the others, before tackling the chaos on her desk. That accomplished, she went to kneel on the floor to check through the two boxes of glassware that lay there unopened, wincing slightly as a familiar ache throbbed through her thigh. But the heady scent from the climbing wisteria outside the window, perfuming the tranquil night air, immediately distracted her, and the tune that Laura had been contentedly humming turned into a fully-fledged song.

As Fabian walked into the softly lit marble-floored hallway of the villa all the hairs on the back of his neck stood on end. The voice he could hear singing was so delightful, so exquisitely pure, that he just stood where he was listening, hardly daring to even breathe. *Who was this angel?* He had never heard her sing before, of that he was certain. Such a voice one would not soon forget! Perhaps she was a younger, more recently recruited member of the company?

As the last notes of the song clung, quivering, to the hushed atmosphere of the night, Fabian let out his breath and moved his head in mute astonishment. He simply had to meet her!

Following the direction whence the voice had come, he walked down the wide, gleaming corridor of closed doors. Everything was absolutely still, with no indication of anyone else's presence. Knocking at each door before he entered a particular room, he called out, *'Ciao? C'e nessuno li?'* Is there anybody there? But every room he visited was empty of any other human being but him.

Had he imagined what he'd just heard? Ridiculous! Clearly one of the company was rehearsing somewhere in private and he had unwittingly disturbed them. He would make it his mission to find them, offer his sincere apologies then introduce himself.

A few minutes later Fabian went still as a statue as the exquisite voice he had heard sounded on the air again. He made his way to the office that Laura was now occupying instead of Carmela. There was a tension inside him that seemed to build with every step. Entering the room, he saw his temporary assistant with her back to him, straightening some files on a bookshelf. He saw she had dispensed with her shoes and her feet were bare, and her previously bound hair fell softly around her shoulders. But most of all he realised that the amazing voice that he was hearing belonged to *her*.

A sense of shock interwoven with pleasure electrified Fabian's spine. He said nothing—he fully intended to let her finish the song before addressing her—but all of a sudden she stopped, turned round, and gazed at him with a slightly stunned expression.

'Oh!'

'Your voice is exquisite… I had no idea.'

'I hope I didn't disturb you? I was just enjoying being here in your beautiful house, and I let my happiness and pleasure spill over. I always sing when I'm happy.'

'Do not apologise. That is a remarkable talent you have, Laura. Carmela never mentioned that you could sing.'

'I last saw her about ten years ago. Although we kept in touch we never really talked about things like that. Besides…it's just something I do to amuse myself these days. Nothing more.'

Her hand slid over her cheekbone and he glimpsed a silver earring with a small pale blue stone shimmering on her lobe as she tucked her hair behind her ear. Fabian could hardly believe she was so dismissive of a talent that other people would trade their life savings for.

'Why is that?' he asked immediately. 'With the right people to guide you, you could have an impressive career. I have been around singers, musicians, artists all my life…I do not say this lightly.'

'But I don't want an impressive career! What I want is to be able to teach music to children, like I was doing before. I would do it for *nothing* if I could afford to!'

Stunned by such an unexpected and passionate response, Fabian lifted his brows in surprise. It was no exaggeration to say that people these days seemed to idolise fame and fortune, and yet this slender reed of a girl—although she clearly had talent in abundance—appeared to scorn it in preference to teaching children! He hadn't felt so taken aback or intrigued by someone in a very long time. Certainly his ex-wife would never have displayed such altruism or heartfelt generosity. Just the opposite, in fact!

But Fabian didn't want to think about the avaricious and deceitful Domenica. Right now it was *this* woman who had all his attention.

'If you would do what you love to do for nothing that is an admirable quality indeed…if a little naïve. You do realise you could very quickly become quite wealthy with a voice like yours, Laura? You would never have to worry about money again.'

'I told you.' Moving across the room, she bent down to collect her discarded sandals, and after sliding her small elegant feet inside the soft brown leather she straightened and rested her gaze directly on Fabian. 'I'm not interested in a career as a singer. I had that dream a long time ago, when I was young, but I've since found something I feel far more passionate about. It may never make me rich, but then wealth doesn't have the fascination for me that it does for some people. Not everyone is so enthralled by the idea of it!' She bit her lip in sudden anxiety. 'I'm sorry. I didn't mean any offence.'

'None taken.'

'My needs are simple…that's all I meant. I think I'll say goodnight now, if you don't mind? I want to make an earlier start tomorrow.'

'You have already worked a long day. There is no need to make an earlier start than normal.'

'If you say so.'

'What about the man in your life? Surely he would want you to make the most of your exceptional talents?'

Fabian was fishing unashamedly, and for a moment Laura appeared dazed by his question.

'I'm a single woman. There is no man in my life apart from my father.'

'Even so…surely he must—?'

'He only wants whatever makes me happy.'

Her small chin came up, and her pale eyes signalled such defiance that Fabian glimpsed unexpected steel in her character that warned him this was as far as he should go right now.

Unable to think of any other reason to keep her there right then, he slid his hand into his trouser pocket and briefly inclined his head. 'Then I will see you in the morning, Laura. Sleep well.'

'And you.'

Her moonlit gaze withdrew, and she slipped past him like the brush of silk against bare skin—the air she left behind intoxicatingly and beguilingly scented with a perfume that was both sultry and innocent at the same time. For a long time after Fabian's feet claimed the same spot on the carpet, as though welded there…

'The lanterns need to be arranged in the trees on either side of the road, so that the drive is clearly lit when people arrive.'

In the middle of explaining some of the external decorating requirements in an earnest blend of English and Italian to the two cheerful and willing workmen standing in the office with her, Laura gave only a perfunctory glance at her boss as he came in through the door, bringing his cup of coffee with him.

From today, she was in *his* domain, and she had never before set foot in such a plush, richly decorated office.

It was nearly twice the size of Carmela's and—along with the crystal chandelier that hung suspended from the cathedral-like ceiling—it was full of the most exquisite art and *objets d'art*. Earlier, the same workmen who were with her now had moved her desk and computer to the opposite side of the palatial room from Fabian, and another young man had appeared to connect everything up again. Sunlight streamed in through the enormous windows as though it were worshipping at a shrine.

She couldn't deny her stomach had flooded with butterflies at the idea that they would be working together so closely. And she couldn't help but recall what had happened last night when Fabian had discovered her singing. She'd been taken aback by the compliments he had paid her on her voice, and the suggestion that she could have a lucrative career out of it, but it had done nothing to change Laura's mind about the career she desperately wanted to resume… that of working with children. Her singing had been a spontaneous, unplanned event, brought about by a contentment she had not experienced in a long time, and she had not sought or expected an audience, much less acknowledgement!

'*Buongiorno!*'

He included everyone in the convivial greeting as

he went to his desk and set down his coffee cup, nonetheless Fabian's glance came to rest specifically on Laura. It was a feat quite beyond her to glance away from the ocean of achingly vivid blue that blazed back at her.

'You slept well?' he asked her.

'Fine, thank you... You?'

'Like a *bambino*!'

His lips broke into the most boyish and captivating grin Laura had ever seen. The sun pouring in through the huge windows behind him illuminated him in a dazzling aura of gold. She knew she was staring, but she would defy anyone—man, woman or child—not to do the same.

'Really?' she murmured.

'Last night I heard an angel singing.' The expression on Fabian's face was deliberately provocative, and it made Laura's skin heat and her heart race. It seemed to suggest that they shared a *secret*...a secret that placed her in his power somehow. 'Yes...I went to sleep with the sound of her exquisite voice lingering tantalisingly in my ears...*bella*!' He kissed his fingers in an extravagant gesture and his smile grew even wider.

The two workmen grinned hugely at this, nodding in vicarious appreciation. Meanwhile, Laura's whole body was trembling so hard she felt sure everyone must see it.

'Yesterday the house was full of so much beautiful music.' Forcing herself to smile nonchalantly, she returned her attention to the waiting workmen, because it was far safer than allowing herself to be caught up in the dangerous spell that Fabian seemed to cast so easily. Striving to maintain an even, slightly authoritative tone in her voice, she crossed her arms in front of her chest. 'Now, you know what's to be done? The lanterns are all ready and waiting in the storeroom. They arrived yesterday, and I've checked that we received the right number. When the job is completed I'll come and have a look. *Grazie.*'

'*Si, signorina.*'

The room fell silent again after the workmen's departure, and Fabian dropped thoughtfully down into his seat. Running his critical gaze over his assistant's porcelain skin and willowy form, he noted that she was looking almost as pale as the marble of one of Michelangelo's sculptures this morning. *Had his teasing upset her?* Hearing her sing was the first thing he had thought about that morning on waking, and he had been thinking about it ever since.

'Why didn't you join me for breakfast?' he asked.

'Maria very kindly brought some coffee and fruit to my room.'

'Coffee and fruit? Are you trying to starve yourself? No wonder you are so slender!'

'I assure you there is nothing wrong with my appetite, Signor Moritzzoni! I enjoy my food just like anyone else! This just happens to be my natural build.'

'No doubt many women would envy you.'

Even as he made the comment, Fabian knew his own preference usually ran to the more voluptuous feminine form. Yet he could not deny that Laura's small frame was perfect for her fine, delicate bone structure.

'I doubt it. I am well aware of how I look, and there is hardly anything to envy.'

Surprised by her self-deprecating reply, Fabian did not believe she'd said it to elicit his protest to the contrary. Yet he could not help but find it a puzzle that she seemed not to realise her own attraction. After all…a scar was just a scar. To him it hardly signified at all, yet he understood that for a woman it might not prove so easy to bear in the looks-obsessed culture that they lived in. About to turn away from her, he saw that she now had two spots of colour in her otherwise still pale cheeks.

'Anyway…I promise I will make up for my small breakfast by eating a good lunch, so you need not worry that I might faint from hunger at your feet, Signor Moritzzoni!'

'That would definitely *not* be good for my reputation, Laura,' he answered dryly. 'And, please…it is about time you started to call me Fabian. Formality only gets in the way when we are working so closely together.'

'If that's what you prefer. Now, there are a couple of things I need to ask you concerning the supper party after the concert.' Turning back to her desk, she picked up a sheaf of paper and a pen.

There was something quite irresistible about the expression she got on her face whenever she was concentrating, Fabian realised. It had the strange effect of making all his muscles tighten with what he had to acknowledge was most assuredly sensual pleasure. He clenched his jaw a little as she approached. Her captivating summery scent reached him first, and he was genuinely perturbed that his reaction to her was so acute. It was an unexpected discovery that could no doubt lead to some unnecessary complications if not handled correctly.

'What is it you want to know?' he asked, frowning.

'It's about the protocol for the evening.'

To his further discomfiture, she came round to stand by his side, then crouched down low, so that he could clearly see the list of invitees with their various titles and designations. But all Fabian could really focus on right then was how her hair seemed to be woven through with dancing sunlight, and how with her small straight nose and delicate jaw her profile was like the most exquisite cameo...

'*Si.*' Taking the list out of Laura's hands, Fabian heard the dismissive tone in his voice. 'I will make some notes in English at the side of each name for you. In the meantime I have some important phone calls to make. This afternoon after lunch we will go through the entire plan and programme together, and find out exactly the state of play.'

'That would be good. Thank you.'

He had said to Carmela that he hoped his new assistant would not expect him to hold her hand or guide her step by step, yet here he was—her desk conveyed to his office and a strangely inexplicable impulse in him not to leave her to cope on her own…

Moving away from him, she suddenly paused. 'Your father must have loved music very much…and this is such an exquisite setting for such an event. Was it your idea to hold a concert in his memory each year?'

Stunned by the question, Fabian stared hard at Laura. A muscle throbbed in his cheek and for a long moment he struggled to stem the swift tide of resentment that flowed through his bloodstream. 'Music meant a lot to him, yes. He considered himself an avid aficionado of the opera. He considered himself an expert in many things as a matter of fact! But holding the concert was not my idea. Far from it! My father left instructions in his will. Even in death, Roberto Moritzzoni wanted to ensure that he was not forgotten. He did not easily let go of his possessions or his life.'

'I see.'

'I doubt that you do, Laura. But perhaps one day before you leave the Villa De Rosa…I will explain.'

Moving his coffee cup out of the way, Fabian concentrated his focus on the list of dignitaries in front of him. They were all—with the exception of some of the key performers in the concert—ex cohorts of his father's who still 'milked' their association with Roberto Moritzzoni for all it was worth. As if they had not dined in the style of kings enough throughout the years at the expense of Fabian's family! At that moment he honestly felt like putting a lighted match to that damned list and having done with it. Glancing up, he saw that Laura had quietly made her way back to her desk, her attention captured by whatever was on the computer screen in front of her. What would Roberto have said if Fabian had introduced someone like *her* to him as his wife-to-be? He could hear the old man's mocking laughter even now, after all these years, at the thought that he would even entertain such an absurdity! Everything about her would have been wrong, he realised—starting with the fact that she was not Italian. Add to that the probability that she had no important or useful family connections—that would be two more strikes against her suitability. As for her looks and figure—Roberto would no doubt have disparagingly dismissed her as too pale, too thin, and not maternal or voluptuous enough to be the bearer of his grandchildren…

'Bigoted old fool!' he muttered savagely beneath his breath.

'Is something the matter?' At the other side of the sun-filled room, Laura studied him in surprise. 'You seem upset,' she pressed, when he did not immediately reply.

'You are right. I *am* upset. Thinking about my father usually ensures that reaction. He was not the most—shall we say…pleasant of men, Laura. He could be quite cruel in fact…*especially* to those that were closest to him. Does that shock you?'

Her sweetly shaped mouth turned down a little and her big eyes looked concerned. 'Cruelty always shocks me…even though I know it is hardly rare in the world.'

Fabian grimaced. 'Then let us change the subject and think about something more pleasant. If you want to restore my good mood, perhaps you would be kind enough to go and get me some more coffee?'

'Of course. I'll go and find Maria and get you some.'

She was on her feet immediately, her shy gaze touching him briefly as she left the room, and as Fabian watched her go he was filled with a longing that he didn't dare examine too closely. The kind of longing that could definitely play havoc with their fledgling boss/secretary relationship.

CHAPTER FOUR

Some of Fabian's well-heeled friends turned up unexpectedly for lunch, and he insisted that Laura join them. They ate *al fresco*, at a table on another spectacular terrace overlooking a lush sea of olive groves. The sun shone and the wine flowed, and although her boss showed an interest in the conversations that went on around him—even occasionally laughing or smiling with his companions—Laura detected that his mind was not entirely focused on the present.

As she cut a sweet red apple into neat quarters and bit into one, she recalled his surprising comments about holding the concert in his father's memory. The revelation that he had been a cruel man *had* disturbed her—mostly because of how that must have affected the young Fabian, growing up. Now that she'd gleaned his relationship with Roberto had been less than idyllic—and that obviously this concert held in his memory was reminding him of the fact—she wasn't surprised that Fabian's thoughts appeared to be elsewhere. She couldn't begin to imagine the money, time and effort it took to organise one of these impressive events—and how much must he be resenting that if it was something he did out of duty and not love? Could it be that he was willing the whole event to be over instead of anticipating it with pleasure?

Her curiosity and concern deepening, Laura lifted her gaze—only to find it on a collision course with Fabian's. Next to her, an Italian count with an unpronounceable name laughed hard at a joke he had made—but she barely registered the sound because once again she'd dived into that flawless blue ocean and found herself short on oxygen. Expecting him to say something, she was honestly deflated when he didn't, but simply glanced away again and started talking to the elderly gentleman beside him.

'*Lo zio*, Fabian!'

A small girl with glossy brown pigtails and eyes the colour of luscious cocoa appeared at the top of the terrace steps, ran towards the table and climbed onto Fabian's lap. Weaving her sturdy brown arms around his neck, she buried her head into his chest.

'Cybele!'

There followed an affectionate demonstration of delight bar none from Fabian, and Laura watched him make a fuss of the child with a sense of almost dizzying surprise and pleasure that she couldn't deny. They made the most compelling tableau—the man with the kind of masculine beauty that would haunt you to your grave and the enchanting dark-haired child—and an old longing swept through her heart and made her want to weep, because she knew it would probably never be realised. *A longing that had been almost utterly destroyed by a relationship turned dramatically wrong.*

Everyone around the table was either applauding or making some admiring comment about the child's beauty and their host's obvious pleasure in her company. Simply for being herself, the child commanded all their attention. But that was just as it should be Laura thought smiling.

'*Scusa*, Signor Morittzoni?'

Now Maria appeared at the top of the steps, puffing and clearly out of breath in her sombre black dress, a delicate lace handkerchief mopping the perspiration that beaded her brow. From what followed, Laura gathered that Cybele was her grandchild, come for a visit. Delighted to learn that Fabian was home, she had rushed ahead to find him.

Fabian told Maria not to worry. He was more than happy to see the child, and asked if she would like to stay and have some food with them. Maria thanked him, but insisted that Cybele go with her and let the grown-ups enjoy their meal in peace. The child went reluctantly, waving goodbye until she and her grandmother finally disappeared from view.

'What a gorgeous little girl!' Laura remarked.

'You like children, *signorina*?' The elderly man next to Fabian leant towards her across the table, the thin, faintly bloodless lips beneath his military-style moustache curving in a knowing smile.

'Yes, I do. Very much.'

'Then you will make a perfect *mamma*! But first you need a husband, *si*?'

There was a chorus of approving laughter, and as Laura tried to field the wave of embarrassment that swept over her at suddenly being the centre of so much attention Fabian's penetrating gaze seared into hers with undisguised interest. But he said nothing.

'Put everything on hold for while…we are going out.'

Re-entering the office after a short but necessary meeting with Maria and her kitchen staff—Laura stared at Fabian in surprise. She got the distinct sense that he'd been pacing and thinking hard about something in her absence, and the tousled appearance of his golden hair indicated he'd tunnelled his impatient fingers through it several times.

'Where?'

'I am taking you to visit the hospice that the concert is being held in aid of. It will be a good opportunity for you to see for yourself the necessity for such a valuable organisation to continue to receive our help.'

'Well, then…' She hovered in the doorway, taken aback by the impromptu nature of this planned visit, as well as by the overwhelming idea of seeing children who were suffering and sick and in some cases dying. Already Laura's senses were clamouring in sympathy and trepidation. 'If you just give me a minute I'll go and get my jacket.'

She hardly registered the helicopter ride to the simple whitewashed group of buildings set deep in the Tuscan hillside. During the short journey, both she and Fabian had lapsed into thoughtful silence, mutually respected and understood. She had questions, without a doubt—but for now they would have to keep.

On their arrival at the hospice they were greeted by a joyful elderly nun—Sister Agnetha—who welcomed Fabian with a beaming smile and a fiercely affectionate hug. The sight made Laura's legs feel unaccountably wobbly. There was no sense of awkwardness or embarrassment evident in him at all, and his arresting eyes clearly reflected his genuine heartfelt pleasure at the reunion. The man was beginning to intrigue her more and more.

Once inside, they were guided from ward to ward, room to room, and in every case Fabian sat on the edge of the sick child's bed and conversed with him as though he were a personal relative, and the children responded in kind—their delight at seeing him palpable, even though they were so ill. For his part, during those encounters a myriad of emotions crossed his startlingly handsome face. Laura saw sympathy, kindness, humour and love written there. At times during the visit, her heart was so full she could barely speak.

It was well into the evening when they emerged from the hospice, and the night was silky soft and fragrant with the rich natural scent of the stunning Tuscan countryside. Laura couldn't help but think that on such a night all should be well in the world… there shouldn't be innocent children suffering and dying. She bit her lip and could not bring herself to look at Fabian in case he saw her distress. After receiving an affectionate goodbye hug from Sister Agnetha herself she knew her mind and emotions were swamped with impressions and feelings both raw and tender, and her already tenuous grip on her self-control was under serious threat.

'Are you all right?' Fabian asked gruffly at her side in the helicopter, as the powerful rotor blades roared into action and lifted them off the ground.

'Yes, I'm fine,' she said, turning her face away to stare out of the window at the fast disappearing earth below.

There had been babies as well as older children

there. That was the sight that had almost completely undone her. What was the point of such short desperate lives full of suffering? She could only imagine what agony their parents were going through. Yet the staff at the hospital had been full of smiles and humour, and some of the less ill children had responded with ready laughter to Fabian's teasing and joking around. This side of his character had been a wonderful revelation to Laura, and she was still reeling from the evidence of it.

'It is hard the first time to see the little ones in such a condition,' he said thoughtfully, his voice raised to compete with the almost deafening sound of the rotor blades. 'But they are so brave...so strong. The least we can do is make sure that they have every facility and comfort available to alleviate their situation as much as possible. Here...'

Finding a large white handkerchief pressed into her hand, Laura dabbed disconsolately at the tears she suddenly couldn't hold back, vaguely aware of the scent of Fabian's arresting cologne on the soft linen square crumpled in her palm. Still she couldn't speak.

'It is late and we have not yet eaten. I will get the pilot to take us to one of my favourite little restaurants so we can have dinner and talk...*si*?'

She managed a nod and the wobbliest of smiles.

The smile Fabian delivered to her in return stole her breath away with the sheer dazzling power of its beauty and warmth.

'You were so easy with the children…so natural.' Laying down her fork on the pristine tablecloth, Laura held his gaze almost reluctantly.

Fabian sensed she was still self-conscious about the emotional response that she hadn't been able to contain during and after their visit to the hospice, but her reaction only confirmed to him that she would make the most caring of mothers herself. The thought was at the forefront of his mind when he finally responded to her quiet observation.

'It is not difficult to be oneself with children, no? They are just themselves, and so that makes it easy. And these particular little ones are such an example of courage and strength in the face of adversity that it humbles one…it truly does.'

The visit had also reminded him *why* he went on with the concert year after year—even though the event had been instigated by a father who had not been the best of examples, and memories of Fabian's own painful childhood were inevitably stirred by it's existence.

'Clearly you have a great bond with children yourself, Laura… Motherhood is something that you must have considered from time to time?'

Taking a deceptively relaxed sip of the fragrant red wine he had ordered with their meal, he realised that there was definite tension inside him as he awaited her response. A faint becoming flush bloomed on her cheeks as she glanced away from him, and he glimpsed sadness in her eyes before she tore her gaze free to stare out at the twinkling lights of the town below.

Situated on a charming terrace high on the hillside, the restaurant had a view that was breathtaking and magical. The cuisine was also exceptional, which was why it had fast become one of Fabian's favourite places to dine when he was back home.

'Laura?' Knowing he had triggered something hard to bear inside her, he felt the tension in the pit of his stomach grow.

'I would love to be a mother,' she answered quietly, returning her glance warily to his. 'I didn't tell you before but…I was married up until just over two years ago.'

Married? Shock and surprise imploded inside him. Carmela had not acquainted him with such a startling piece of information—but then why should she?

'My husband died. We were in a car accident, and unfortunately he was killed outright.'

'Please accept my condolences.'

Even as he voiced the stilted-sounding words, Fabian duelled with feelings of relief as well as regret that Laura had suffered such a shocking event. Relief that she had survived and—if he was honest—relief that she had a husband no longer…

'Thank you. I wanted children—of course I did. But my husband, he…' She folded her hands on the tablecloth, interlinking her ringless fingers with an agitation she wasn't quick enough to disguise. 'He didn't feel the same way.'

Lifting her glass, she drank some wine, as though striving to contain whatever bruising memories had surfaced inside her. When she returned it to the table again she looked slightly calmer. But Fabian wasn't fooled. It must have been devastating to a woman who loved children as she did to be with a man who had not shared that feeling.

'And the accident did not affect your ability to bear children in the future?' he heard himself ask.

'Thankfully, no. Broken bones…cuts and bruises… that was the extent of my injuries. I'm lucky there was no internal bleeding, or anything that could have caused a major problem.'

She had escaped being killed in a car crash, had lost her husband and been left with physical scars as well as psychological ones, no doubt—and she thought herself lucky?

'I am sorry that I have inadvertently raised a subject that brings you so much pain and sorrow.' His hand moved across the table to cover hers. It was deathly cold. 'The visit to the hospice clearly upset you far more than I had envisaged, but I did not know beforehand that you had your own personal tragedy to endure.'

'How could you have known? But don't think for one second that I regret going. It makes me want to work even harder to help make this concert the very best it can be! Thank you for giving me the opportunity to meet those wonderful children. I'll always remember them.'

'Now you must eat something. Food and wine can help in times like these. And if we do not look as though we are enjoying our meal my good friend Alberto, who owns this restaurant will think we do not like it and will worry that he has done something wrong!'

It wasn't until he glanced downwards that Fabian saw he was still holding Laura's hand, and she had made no move to dislodge it.

She had wondered what Fabian's incredible hands might look like holding a child, and since yesterday at the hospice, and before that with Maria's grand-daughter Cybele, she had seen for herself. Now Laura could hardly get the image out of her mind.

Her thoughts were thus occupied when he came up behind her at the photocopier, and Laura sensed the air crackle with the electricity of his presence. She didn't turn around.

'You are very quiet today. Is anything wrong?'

Pressing the keypad to issue further copies she did not really need, Laura hid behind the confusion of noise to disguise her feelings—disturbing feelings that she barely knew what to do with.

'I'm fine! There's nothing wrong. I'm just concentrating on my work, that's all.'

'You are still perhaps upset at seeing the children yesterday? It is completely understandable and nothing to try and hide.'

To Laura's disconcertment she felt his hands come to rest on either side of her hips, the contact all but burning her through her thin silk dress. Heat descended like soft, intoxicating warm rain on skin laid bare to its touch.

'I like this dress you are wearing,' he murmured softly behind her, his warm breath stirring her loosened hair.

Sucking in her own breath, she felt shock and pleasure roll through her with equal force. He'd already filled her with myriad longings by the touch of his hand holding hers last night at dinner to comfort her, but *this*…this had to be the sweetest, most sensual torment she'd ever experienced!

'It's nothing special.'

'On the contrary. Do you really not realise how enticing it is?'

The touch of his lips at the place where her neck sloped down into her collarbone made Laura gasp out loud. She was glad she was standing next to something she could lean on, because all of a sudden her limbs had no bones to hold her upright.

'Fabian…you shouldn't be—please don't do that!'

With a supreme effort she forced herself to move, to turn around and face him, and was stunned to see the liquid heat that blazed back at her from his azure eyes. A heat that confirmed to her it was *desire* that interested him right now…not the demands of the concert or running his estate or anything else. It had been a long time since Laura had thought of herself as desirable, and it was hard to believe a man like him would look at her that way…as if he could eat her up with just a glance!

'You looked so pretty…so fragile and thoughtful…as you stood there with the sunlight glinting in your hair. I could not resist you!' His fingers tipped up her chin. They were hard, warm and insistent, so that she had no choice but to face him. 'Do not be afraid of me, Laura… I would never do anything to hurt you.'

'I—I know that. Look, I'd really better get back to work. The list of things to do seems to be growing ever longer, and time isn't standing still!'

She broke away from him so abruptly she nearly

fell over a nearby chair, and with her face flaming with embarrassment she bolted from the room before Fabian could stop her.

He had mulled over the stunning and perhaps crazy idea he'd had over and over again until finally— restless and slightly agitated from its relentless demand—he'd left Laura amid the detritus of organisation and gone for a walk.

The Moritzzoni family estate included several hundred acres of fertile land around the villa, and Fabian had headed off deep into the hills, uncaring that the afternoon sun laid its hand upon his unprotected head like an overheated iron. Eventually driven to seeking some shade, he'd dropped down onto his haunches beneath a dense grouping of trees, and now he wiped the sweat from his brow and the back of his neck with an unconnected, distracted air.

A compelling picture stole into his mind...*the soft, melting glance on Laura's face when Cybele had appeared during lunch yesterday*. And when his old friend Lachimo had made that comment about her making a perfect mother Fabian had felt an answering leap of confirmation deep in his gut. Later on in the day, when they'd visited the children at the hospice, another layer of admiration and approval of her maternal instincts had been beguilingly reaffirmed.

Perhaps it wasn't so crazy after all to contemplate

the route that had become almost too persuasive to ignore? If he were going to commit to such an undertaking at all then he would much prefer it to be with a woman who had no connection with his past or his family. That way it would be a completely fresh start for both of them. A woman who genuinely appeared to love children as well as sharing his own passion for music might be persuaded to see that the idea had much to commend it—*despite* her avowed uninterest in wealth. Their partnership would not be complicated or sullied by the kind of emotional entanglement that Fabian wanted to avoid at all costs. Yet there would be physical consolation too. He recalled how aroused he'd been when he'd kissed her neck and felt her delightful body quiver through her thin dress. *What if she really did turn out to be the solution he'd been searching for?*

From the moment he pushed to his feet again and swept his sweat-dampened hair off his brow he had convinced himself that he should not let this potential opportunity to realise the thing he wanted most— an *heir*—slip away.

Working late into the evening again, Laura was surprised when Fabian returned to the office to rejoin her after dinner. He had said little during the exceptional *stracotto di fagiano* that Maria had served up for them, and continued to wear that same distracted, pensive air about him that he'd worn yesterday at lunch. Now he paced the floor as Laura endeavoured to tick off the myriad jobs she'd managed to accomplish that day, though it was practically impossible to ignore his eye-catching physique in fawn coloured chinos and sky-blue linen shirt as he walked back and forth in front of her. It was even more impossible not to let her gaze rest upon his perfectly shaped, highly erotic tanned bare feet as he did so…

Withdrawing her fingers from the keyboard, she flexed them a little, sensing a trickle of perspiration meander sluggishly down her back. It was as though invisible strings were pulling her attention back to him every time she tried to look away, and the fact that she couldn't resist played on her mind. *Given that she had made a spectacularly wrong choice about a man once before, her interest troubled her deeply.*

'Is there anything I can do for you?' she asked now, her softly modulated voice sounding almost too loud in the quiet room.

'No.' He stared at her as though in a trance.

'It's just that you seem so—'

'*Si,*' he said abruptly, suddenly approaching her desk and leaning his hands on it.

Suddenly his compelling face was right in front of hers, and Laura saw the shadowed imprint that cleft his strong chin with such definition, and the faint but discernible threads of maturity that waved on his brow. As for his too-disturbing gaze—Laura did her best to skim over it, lest she willingly drown in that perfect river of blue.

'I would like you to take a walk with me.'

'Now?'

'*Si*. You have not had an opportunity to see the grounds properly yet, and we should go before the light dies. Fetch a wrap or shawl, if you have one, and I will meet you at the front entrance.'

In the end, it didn't matter that it was almost dusk. Nearly everywhere Laura glanced were softly glowing lanterns and fairy lights, and the extensive grounds of the impressive Villa de Rosa took on a quality of enchantment that would ensure she never forgot the breathtaking impression it made for as long as she lived.

'We will stop here for a moment.'

Fabian touched her arm and Laura sensed the contact sear through the delicate lace of her antique shawl, permeate her skin and reach down inside the very marrow in her bones. Ever since he'd kissed her neck she was like the most inflammable tinder to his touch. All her defences seemed to be in tatters where he was concerned.

They were standing by a weathered wooden bench positioned against an aging brick wall, and the glorious scarlet bougainvillaea that tumbled over it sang its seductive perfume to the gentle night air.

'We will sit for a while.'

'Something is bothering you, isn't it? Is it anything to do with the organisation of the concert?'

'No. I can see that you have everything under control where that is concerned, and I am impressed by what you have accomplished so far and your dedication to doing a good job.'

As he laid his hand on her knee, she saw the stunning gold and emerald signet ring on his little finger glint in the softly diffused light.

'Then what is it?'

'I have been thinking that we should get to know each other a little better.'

Hardly prepared for such a statement, Laura stayed quiet. But, even so, wave upon wave of heat coursed through her in a seemingly unstoppable flow.

'What I mean is, this is a good opportunity for us to talk. Why don't you start by telling me a little bit more about yourself? I know that you went to school with Carmela in London, that you have the most surprisingly angelic voice and have a passion for teaching music to children. What else?'

Laura's mind seemed to freeze for a moment. Telling him more about herself would inevitably bring up the past again, and she'd really like to avoid that if she could.

'Laura?' His voice was edged with slight impatience.

'I was just thinking. What kind of things would you like to know?'

As soon as the question left her lips she knew it was the wrong one. She'd been trying to buy time and it had backfired on her. Now she'd left herself wide open, perhaps to some too dangerous examination.

'You said that your husband did not feel the same you did about having children? Will you tell me why?'

'Why?' Her temples throbbed with pain.

'Yes—why?'

Her mouth was like a desert as she spoke, and she tried to choose her words carefully. 'Mark was a very jealous man. He said he wanted to have me to himself. He didn't even like me seeing my friends. Children were never going to be on the cards in such an impossible situation.'

'Yet you stayed with him.'

He'd hit the bullseye, and her heart started to thump hard inside her chest. The enchanting night receded, along with the heady scent of flowers and the chorus of insects making their nocturnal sounds in the background.

'Yes…I stayed. Unbelievably, I was married to him for three years.'

'You must have cared deeply for him if you were willing to sacrifice your own need for children to stay with such a man.'

There was a frown on his handsome face, and Laura wondered at the depth of interest in his eyes.

'My feelings for him were…complicated.' Tugging her shawl more securely around her, she felt suddenly far colder than the temperature dictated she should be. The fragrant wind lapped across her body like ice.

'What does that mean, Laura? Tell me.'

Fabian's long, unwavering gaze was like a flame licking at her, and it was hard to hold out against such a compelling force.

'I…I was afraid of him.'

The gaze that scrutinised her features so closely narrowed, then he stared even harder than before. 'Did he intimidate you? Hurt you?'

'Yes.'

'He physically hurt you?'

'Sometimes…yes.'

He bit out something that was clearly a savage expression of disgust. 'I am very sorry to hear you say that. But I am not sorry to hear that such a man is no longer in your life! Accident or not, you are clearly much better off without him!'

Her throat starting to ache, Laura sensed the encroaching tide of anguished memory skirt too close for comfort, and mentally willed it to back off. It was a technique she'd learned to save her sanity. It was rare that she spoke about Mark and his treatment of her—to anyone. Not even her parents. Keeping the wounding memories at bay sometimes felt like a full-time job, but she had no desire to wallow in pain and regret or even self-pity. Time and time again she told herself it was the future she should concentrate on… *not* the past.

'Anyway…it's a part of my life I try not to think about too often. I'm sure you can understand that? These things can either shape you or break you, and I'd take drastic steps before I let that happen!' A small heartfelt sigh escaped into the fragrant air. 'And what about you, Fabian?' All Laura's muscles clenched hard as she succumbed to her own curiosity about *him*. In the deepening dusk, his arrestingly sculpted face was thrown partly into shadow. Yet still the wariness that he wore like a shield was startlingly evident. 'Presumably…with this estate to run and everything…you would like children too?' she continued.

'I have made you sad, reminding you of the past.' Abruptly getting to his feet, it was clear that Fabian had no intention of answering Laura right then. 'Let us continue our walk, and I promise not to upset you with any more difficult questions…*si*?'

As she stood up, her mind busy with pondering why he could ask her about her desire for children but she could not do the same to him, he put his hand against her back, and once again her skin registered his touch like a ray of heat that scorched right through her clothing to leave her tingling.

'Okay…'

They walked on in silence for a while, and gradually Laura's tension around Fabian began to ebb a little.

'I'm trying to imagine what it must have been like, growing up in a place like this,' she announced suddenly, drinking in the stunning vista all around her. 'Your own enchanted forest!'

'Enchanted?' His voice was devoid of the pleasure she had half expected to hear in it. 'I suppose to someone viewing it from the outside it might look like that.'

His tone hinted at bitterness and regret, and it made Laura wonder about the extent of his father's cruelty. Her chest tightened in sympathy. Instead of pursuing her curiosity about his past, she decided to contain it for another day.

Turning his back, Fabian led her down a narrow winding pathway edged with a riot of colourful exotic blooms, and through an arbour of roses that led into yet another exquisite garden, bursting with colour and scent.

Laura drank it all in—the beauty, the night and the man—and the startling realisation came to her that she longed for these stunning moments never to come to an end.

CHAPTER FIVE

IT MADE sense that she was a widow. What else but a tragedy could have put that distant yet undeniable hurt in her pale grey eyes?

The following afternoon, watching Laura from the long windows of the office as she conversed on the lawn with the catering supervisor of the company they'd hired to provide the food and drink for the concert attendees, Fabian reflected on why he had held back on the proposition he had been going to put to her. *Was two years long enough to get over the death of her husband and the cruel legacy of memory he must have left her with? Had she loved him, despite his cruelty? And had her experience coloured her view of all future possibilities of another relationship?*

Last night had not been the time to quiz her on any of this. But, despite all his unanswered questions, it came to him that under the circumstances she might well welcome a partnership where there was no emotional expectation involved or required other than that she be a devoted mother and the kind of respectful wife whom not a breath of scandal would ever touch to shame him. In return Fabian could give Laura many things that would help make life good for her…a sense of security and stability, for one thing, and a guarantee that both she and their offspring would never want for anything. Would that be enough to persuade her to become his wife?

'I can't believe the concert is tomorrow night! It feels like everything is coming together at last—fingers crossed! And I've a feeling it's going to be just wonderful!'

She breezed into the room, a clutch of papers in a see-through folder against her chest, her hair slightly tousled from the welcome breeze that had sprung up that morning. Fabian glanced up from the list of phone calls he had yet to make and spied a speck of white at the corner of her mouth. Getting to his feet, he wandered across to where she stood and inspected the mark more closely.

'You appear to have some cream at the side of your mouth,' he told her, and before Laura could do anything about it he reached towards her and smoothed it away with his fingers. Her eyes went round as dinner plates.

'Maria gave me some cake a while ago. I should

have checked in a mirror. I've been standing there talking to Signor Minetti from the catering company for the past twenty minutes!'

'It was barely noticeable.' Smiling, Fabian reflected that he liked her confusion, and the way she blushed so readily. But right then he had other, more important considerations to contemplate. His face turned suddenly serious. 'We will take some time out,' he announced, catching her by the elbow and guiding her back to where he'd been working. He nodded towards the padded seat on the other side of the desk that had been left there for visitors. 'Sit down, Laura.'

'Did I tell you that some of the stars from the opera are coming over this evening to rehearse?' she asked him, still clutching the sheaf of papers against her emerald-green dress and clearly nervous.

'Yes, you did…*twice*, as a matter of fact.'

'Oh…' She pursed her lips, then blew out a long breath. It made a silky strand of yellow hair dance across her cheek. 'Maria is organising some refreshments afterwards, and they'd like you to join them. Did I tell you that?'

'I believe I am fully up to date with what is happening this evening, so you do not need to worry.'

'Good…I mean *bene.*'

'Why don't you just try and relax? You seem a little agitated today.'

'I'm not agitated! Just excited, I suppose…about the concert tomorrow, I mean.'

Resting his elbows on the desk with a sigh, Fabian linked his hands together and studied Laura for several seconds before continuing. He told himself he could wait for the right time for ever, so what he had to say might as well be now.

'So…there is another matter I wanted to discuss with you. But first let me ask you how you like the Villa de Rosa and being here in Tuscany?'

'I like it very much. How could anyone *not* like such a place? It's as close to paradise as I can think of!'

It threw Fabian for a minute, the sheer pleasure that her ready, artless smile conveyed. Of course her affirmation was somewhat at odds with his own feelings about the place he'd grown up in—the place that his father had turned into one of the most enviable houses in Italy and been so fiercely possessive of. So much so that he had actively resented passing it on to his son—but Laura did not know that.

'Then it would not be in the realms of impossibility to imagine yourself living here?'

'Are you offering me a permanent position working for you?'

The idea aroused mixed feelings in Laura, although the most prevalent one that she held deep inside her heart was *elation*. She'd so wanted to write a new, positive chapter to her life, and maybe this was the chance she'd been praying for? Fabian's touch still lingered at the side of her mouth, where he'd wiped away the whipped cream Maria's cake had left behind, and an awareness had slowly but surely taken root inside her that she more than liked this man. And that was where her doubts crept in about working for him…

'No. That is not what I am offering you at all!'

His reply was surprisingly terse. Crushing disappointment poured ice water over the joy she'd felt.

'I'm sorry…I didn't mean to assume—'

'There is no need to apologise. Let me not waste any more time getting to the point. I am suggesting a proposition that I would very much like you to give your serious consideration.' He drew his hand across the black open-necked shirt he wore, briefly distracting her. 'You asked me last night whether I wanted children. The answer is yes…*of course*. I need an heir, just like any other man in my position.'

Rubbing the furrow between his brows, he sighed as if he carried the cares of the world on his shoulders.

'Perhaps now would be an appropriate time to tell you that I was also married when I was very young— to a girl I discovered after I had wed her did *not* confine her favours to her husband alone. Her behaviour brought shame on me, and made me realise that I had let my lust for her blind me to other less than desirable qualities of hers. Such a woman was not fit to be a mother, in my opinion, and I had no choice but to divorce her. Since then I have been too preoccupied with work and running this estate to enter into another serious relationship. But in order to have the heir that I wish for I obviously need a wife too. What I am proposing, Laura, is that you enter into a strictly business arrangement with me to achieve both those ends. In return you will lead a comfortable, prosperous life as the mistress of the Villa de Rosa and the mother of my child. You need not ever work again, if you do not wish to—although of course I will honour whatever decision you make in that area, as long as they reasonably fit in with my own.

'You do not have to answer me straight away… you will no doubt wish to take the proper time to think things over before telling me what you have decided. I realise we have only known each other for just a short time, but in that time you have made quite an impression on me. I have learned that you are hard-working and talented, and clearly not motivated by money or fame. You have a quiet, relaxing presence and my staff—especially Maria—are already clearly fond of you. Add to that your obvious regard for children, and Carmela's assurance that you are completely reliable…all these things together are enough to convince me that you and I would work very well together as a couple and make a success of such a marriage.'

It was as though a cyclone had swept through the room and left her stunned and dazed. It had appeared out of nowhere without warning… After such a shocking visit, the room and herself would never be the same again. In contrast, Fabian radiated extreme calm—the absolute antithesis of her own wild tumult.

'I can hardly take it in… Are you being serious?'

The plastic wallet of papers slid out of her grip and onto her lap. She grabbed it just in time before it fell onto the floor.

'Do you think I am making a joke?' He scowled. 'I know my proposition may come as something of a surprise, even a shock, but trust me…I do not come to such decisions lightly or without giving them the proper consideration and thought.'

'But if you are in earnest about such a proposal… why pick *me*?'

The tanned skin between Fabian's golden brows tightened perceptibly. 'I have just told you why.'

'Have you? All I heard was a list of my supposed attributes, as though I was some useful household object you were thinking of acquiring! You haven't *begun* to explain your reasons as to why you would want such a strange arrangement!'

'It may seem strange to you, but it is entirely practical in my view. I have told you that I want a family, like any other man in my position, but what I do not want or need is emotional entanglement. I have no illusions about love affairs…none at all! And something as important as marriage should be entered into with a clear head, in my view. Letting emotions dictate your future life with someone, when those very same emotions are merely transient states, only ensures that the outcome will probably be the divorce court! *That* is why I have proposed what I have proposed.'

Laura shivered. 'Transient states? You don't believe that two people can fall in love? That that love might last a lifetime?'

'That is just a foolish hope perpetuated by dreamers. I do not mean to distress you, Laura, but look at your own situation.'

'Just because things turned out the way they did with Mark, that doesn't mean that I didn't have hopes once upon a time that we would have a marriage that lasted the test of time!'

'That is just what I mean!'

Her face fell.

'You were still in love with him at the end? Despite his ill treatment of you?'

'No, I wasn't in love with him… But that doesn't mean I'd stopped caring about him! My feelings were confused… Mostly I felt pity for the tormented, disappointed man he'd become…for the reasons he'd let drink get such a hold on him. But that wasn't my point!'

Those wide shoulders of his lifted in a shrug. 'Be

honest with yourself… Under the circumstances, it was not very likely that your marriage would have lasted the test of time. And I am a pragmatist…a realist about life. In my situation I *have* to be.'

'And does your pragmatism extend to the bedroom? Because presumably you *have* realised that having a child together would involve some kind of intimacy? Or am I supposed to visit a clinic and be impregnated from a sample in a test tube?'

His answering expletive was short and sharp. 'Do not insult me! Of course I know what is required, and I do not foresee any difficulty in that area of our marriage. We are young and healthy, and when we are alone together nature will no doubt take its course.'

'Well…' Staring at him as though seeing him for the first time, and hardly able to contain the contradiction of feelings and emotions that coursed through her, Laura rose slowly to her feet. 'You seem to have it all sorted out nicely. I have a question for you, Fabian… Did you think of asking me to enter into this marriage with you because you think a man *couldn't* fall in love with a woman like me? A woman with a difficult marriage in her past, that literally ended in disaster, as well as a disfiguring scar?'

'Your scar does not make you any less attractive! Surely you must know that? And as for your marriage—you are right. It is in the past! It does not mean that you cannot make better choices in the present! Choices that will enhance your life and not impede it. I would not treat you cruelly, Laura… you have my word on that. And I would give you the children we *both* desire! Is that really so abhorrent?'

She felt so torn. It was becoming extremely clear to Laura that the more time she spent with Fabian, the more attached to him she would become. But he had as good as told her she could never hope for him to love her. Yet the idea of bearing his children—children she already knew she would love and protect with everything that was in her—was anything *but* abhorrent! Could she really compromise her own need for love to enter into a marriage of convenience with this man? But then she'd married Mark because she'd believed he loved her and would never willingly hurt her. See where that mistaken thinking had got her!

Her breath was exhaled in the longest sigh. 'I will think about your proposal. That's all I can say about it right now. But just to let you know…even though my first marriage failed—rightly or wrongly—I still have the idea that marriage should involve a lot more than clear-headed logic! Perhaps I am one of those foolish dreamers that you so disdain? Excuse me. I should get back to work now. The opera company are coming this evening and I—'

'I am pleased that you are prepared to think over my offer. I really believe that when you have considered all the facts you will see the sense and opportunity in it, Laura. And, if you accept, it will bring more benefits to you than you realise.'

Suddenly he was in front of her, his spicy cologne, blazing blue eyes and the heat emanating from his body crowding her senses and knocking down every one of her poorly equipped defences against him. Laura clung onto the sheaf of papers she held against her chest as though it was some kind of lifeline, thrown to her in the midst of a choppy ocean where she was under dire threat of drowning. He moved, and suddenly his long cool palms were enclosing the tops of her arms. She fought with everything she had to try and desensitise herself against his touch, but that was an outcome that was doomed to failure from the moment he'd stepped close.

Her lower lip quivered helplessly. 'Please…let me go. I can't afford to waste any more time this afternoon.'

When Laura thought Fabian was going to release her, he shockingly outwitted her. Almost before she realised what was happening his hands had locked tight around her arms, his chest pressed against hers—and he kissed her. Scorching heat spread over the tender skin of her mouth and consumed her in a sensual conflagration. If she were a forest, she would be charred wood and ashes by now. Making a small husky sound of need in her throat, she let his tongue invade her, and willingly drowned in a sea of hot masculine demand that drove away every ounce of caution and doubt completely.

Seconds ticked by in languorous slow motion, and Laura entered a world of the senses she'd only guessed existed before now. Somehow his fingers were sliding over her scalp, pushing through the tousled strands of her yellow hair with destroying erotic ease and the mercenary kiss—because she didn't doubt that was what it was—deepened and made her shake. The wallet of papers slid unheeded to the floor, and she held on to his lean hard torso so that she wouldn't lose her balance. Having no head for heights, she knew of the debilitating effects of vertigo, but this feeling of utter disorientation was even more terrifying.

'You see?' Fabian drawled, provocatively disengaging his sensual lips from hers, his clear blue gaze slightly amused. 'There is nothing to fear about intimacy between us. We will do very well in that regard, as I already knew we would. Now, as delightfully distracting as this is, we do—as you so rightly said—need to get back to work. I think we will talk about this matter again after the concert…agreed?'

Amid the laughter and sense of heightened anticipation that hung in the air of the luxurious salon on the eve of the anniversary concert, where his elegantly attired guests were enjoying the champagne, bowls of lush Tuscan olives and delicious antipasti that Maria and her kitchen staff had provided for the occasion, Fabian found himself from time to time thinking about the sensual impact of the kiss that he and Laura had shared. His skin prickled with sultry demanding heat every time he did so.

The kind of convenient marriage he had proposed to her would have its compensations, he discovered. It would not hurt that he was physically attracted to her and she to him. *Oh how he had felt the violent tremors pulsing through her body as he held her!* In light of his need for an heir, this was a positive plus! Yet she had been so quiet all the rest of that afternoon—her attention consumed by the demands of the concert, only speaking to Fabian when she absolutely had to. The heightened anticipation that he personally was going through was not about the coming performance tomorrow night, but about the final answer that Laura had promised she would give him concerning his proposal.

A world-famous tenor was shaking his hand and talking about the last time they'd met in Rome for lunch, saying they should do it again soon. Fabian hardly heard him, he was so caught up in his own distracting thoughts. Where was she? He glanced round the room across the big man's shoulder. She'd still been at work when he'd left the office earlier, to go and get ready for the evening, but surely she had finished what she'd been doing by now? She had better put in an appearance soon, because he needed her here to help entertain his guests. He had noted how good Laura was at putting people at their ease, despite not being totally fluent in the language.

When she did arrive, she slid into the room almost unnoticed amid the melee of people. Fabian registered her appearance with relief and then curiosity. Wearing a demure long-sleeved cream smock with white palazzo pants—her expression a little guarded—she did not look as relaxed as she might. It was the sultriest of evenings, and most of the other females in the room were attired in far more revealing outfits in comparison.

Laura always seemed to be intent on covering up, Fabian noticed. Was she really so painfully self-conscious about her own slender form? When they were married, he would have to see what he could do about that. Perhaps when they shared a bed together he would teach her to be less self-conscious, even proud of what Mother Nature had gifted her with? The highly charged thought revived the languorous heat in his body, and he realised he was very close to being aroused.

Having wished his final guest farewell, Fabian returned to the salon to find Laura chatting to Maria as the housekeeper and two of her young staff began the clear-up after the drinks party. After congratulating the older woman on a job well done, and sharing a gentle good-humoured joke, he drew Laura out onto the moonlit veranda through the opened patio doors to talk to her.

'You handled that very well tonight. Several of my guests commented on how charming you were,' he told her, opening the single button on his stylish sports jacket to reveal the perfectly smooth black T-shirt he wore underneath.

'So many well-known faces from the world of opera!' she breathed, waving her hand in front of her too-warm face. 'I'm not generally starstruck, but I had to pinch myself one or two times to convince myself it wasn't all a dream!'

'I think they would have been even more impressed with *you* if they had had the privilege of hearing you sing.'

'With *their* phenomenal talent? No way! That would be like comparing a thoroughbred race horse to a nag.' Folding her arms across her chest, Laura grimaced self-deprecatingly.

'A nag?'

'A horse that's been put out to grass…a non-starter.'

'Why do you underestimate your talents so? I do not understand.'

'Perhaps it's just the way we Brits look at life. We don't believe in getting above ourselves.'

'And I do not believe in such ridiculous false modesty! When you have a talent—and a talent such as yours—you should be proud, not act as though you are embarrassed about it and try to hide it away!'

Studying those faintly disapproving lips of his, Laura remembered the languid, earth-shattering kiss they'd shared earlier—though it was true to say it had been almost constantly on her mind ever since…that *and* Fabian's startling proposition. Now, because of it, she had the sense of tumbling at speed down a steep rocky incline, with no prospect of anything to halt her flight except even more rocks.

'I have no illusions about love affairs…none at all', he'd almost violently asserted, and she had known in that instant that his ex-wife's betrayal had destroyed his faith in love. He'd never got it back. Secretly her heart went out to him, but she had been hurt too—and badly—yet she knew she had not surrendered all hope of loving and being loved again.

'Returning to the concert,' he said now, rubbing his hand round his strikingly sculpted, smoothly shaved jaw. 'I want you front of house with me, and I also want you to announce the performers.'

'What?'

'You have earned the right, Laura.'

His voice had all the fiercely powerful magic of a

tropical moonlit night enfolding her, and he slid his hand underneath the weight of her hair and stroked the side of her neck. The melting, liquid feeling this induced was turning her bones to rubber again, and she opened her grey eyes very wide as her gaze spilled into his. She knew she should pull away, put some distance between them to show him she wasn't going to fall like some windfall apple right into his hands, but somehow she couldn't bring herself to do it.

'I've only done the job you hired me to do,' she replied quietly. 'And perhaps you'd better stop touching me like this…somebody might see.'

'I have made you an offer of marriage, Laura. Do you think that when my staff know that they will be surprised that I want to touch you?'

At his unexpected, somewhat provocative answer, Laura finally found the will to withdraw from him. 'In your own words, you have made me a business proposition—and now you're acting like it's a real marriage you're proposing!'

'When we are married, it *will* be a real marriage—in almost every sense.'

'Will it? That's not the impression I got at all.' Shivering, Laura turned her back on him, so that he wouldn't see the sudden glimmer of moisture in her eyes. *He* might believe he could live without love, but she knew differently. To exist without love meant you were consigning yourself to only half a life.

After what she had been through and survived, she wanted so much more than that. 'And you're talking like my mind has been made up, as if I've already agreed to your proposal, when I haven't!'

'Then I apologise, if you think I am putting unfair pressure on you.' Fabian's hands were on her shoulders, turning her back to face him. There was a slight shift of awareness in his expression—almost surprise—as he registered her emotion. 'I will wait for your answer until after the concert, as we agreed.'

The white diaphanous curtains at the patio doors blew up in a sudden fierce gust, and the tension in the air seemed to thicken. 'I think we're going to have rain tonight,' Laura murmured, her blood heating because he was touching her again. 'Maybe even a storm.' Mark's touch had never made her feel like this…not even at the beginning of their marriage. And in the end…she'd hardly been able to bear him touching her at all…

'If you are frightened of storms, my bedroom is just along the corridor from yours, Laura.'

'I'm not frightened of them,' she said, slipping out of his grasp and running her hand over her hair. 'I *like* them, as a matter of fact! I'm feeling extremely tired all of a sudden…I need to turn in. I'll see you in the morning.'

'By the way… Before you go, you will need a gown for tomorrow…something beautiful and elegant to wear. I have asked a good friend of mine who is a designer in Milano to bring a selection for you to choose. I have guessed your size, and I pride myself on having a very good eye for detail.'

Feeling surprise and heat throb through her at the idea that he'd been studying her figure and estimating her size, Laura stared. 'You didn't need to do that!'

'*Si*...I did. This event is going to be a glittering, fashionable affair, and I would not have my hostess for the evening dressed in anything less than *haute couture*!'

'Yes, but I wish you'd mentioned all this before, Fabian. I don't think I'm entirely comfortable with the idea of being on show—not to mention standing up in front of all those important people and announcing the performers! That's definitely something I didn't expect!'

'You seem to persist in wanting to hide yourself!' His tone exasperated, Fabian glowered. 'Your body, your talent... What else will you try to hide from me, Laura?'

Immediately thinking of Mark—of *why* he had crashed their car that dreadful night—Laura felt her blood suddenly run as cold as the grave, and her hand visibly shook as she smoothed it down over the front of her cream top.

'Goodnight, Fabian.' She brushed past him before he could try and waylay her.

CHAPTER SIX

'LAURA? This is my good friend Dante Pasolini. He has brought some gowns for you to try on.'

Persuading Laura away from work this morning had not been easy, Fabian found. Certainly her dedication and conscientious approach to the task in hand was not to be faulted, yet he could hardly suppress the impatience that arose inside him at her reluctance to even look at the beautiful dresses that Dante had selected at Fabian's request. Now, as she stretched out her hand to greet the older man, she was clearly taken aback when the stylishly dressed Maestro of Italian *haute couture* kissed her soundly on both cheeks, then held her away from him, so that he could run his expert gaze up and down her figure.

'But she is perfect, Fabian!' he announced in English. 'Like a young Grace Kelly! You have made my task very easy today. Come, *signorina*—my

Aladdin's Cave of exquisite delights awaits you! Fabian, *per favore*, wait here and we will present my selection to you one by one.'

Immediately Fabian saw how uncomfortable Laura was with this idea—but he would not accede to her discomfort and go away. He was just like any other Italian when it came to beautiful things, and he was intrigued to see this private little fashion parade Dante had in store. So he took up residence in a high-backed armchair in the luxurious salon that overlooked the blaze of elegant white marquees glinting in the sunshine, and ignored Laura's silent plea.

There was a small vestibule, and then another room leading off that, which was where Dante had set up his rail of stunning dresses. As he watched the two of them disappear, Fabian mulled over the coming concert, sensing the old resentment towards his father return. He should have brought the event to an end a long time ago because of the distress it caused him, but he'd resisted because of the substantial amounts of money it raised for the children's hospice. If it weren't for that, it would no longer be the one uncomfortable sticking point in his calendar.

He wasn't afraid of *not* carrying out to the letter the instructions in Roberto's will. After all...what could his despotic tyrannical spirit do? Haunt him from the grave? Yet after their visit to the hospice, and engaging with those incredible children again, Fabian knew he would not call a halt to the yearly concerts. Scraping his hand resignedly through his hair, he turned his mind instead towards the future for a moment. With a sudden great yearning he thought about what his own children would be like when he became a father. He did not doubt they would help bring more meaning and purpose to his life…something he had been craving for a very long time. Work, money, admiration—these were empty pursuits in comparison, and the satisfaction in all of them momentary and fleeting.

Caught up in his thoughts, it took him a couple of seconds to register the fact that Dante was at the door gesturing to him with what was definitely a worried expression on his face. In a torrent of concerned Italian, the older man told him what was the problem. His stomach gripped with disquiet, Fabian followed him back into the room he had just vacated.

Laura stood at the tall Palladian window with her back to him. She was dressed in a full-length scarlet backless gown that displayed to perfection the long slim lines of her body, notwithstanding the feminine curves that were the epitome of grace rather than voluptuous. For a moment he was spellbound. With her soft halo of bright hair and pearlescent skin, he knew she would elicit many appreciative admiring gasps in such a gown. Yet as he moved towards her he could tell that she was deeply upset. Thinking of what his friend had told him, he took a steadying breath.

'Laura?'

'This is far too revealing,' she said, in a voice thickened by emotion. 'I couldn't possibly wear such a dress in public.'

Laying his hands on her shoulders, Fabian slowly made her turn round to face him. 'My only wish is that you feel beautiful in whatever gown you ultimately choose. I would not wish for one moment for you to wear anything that makes you remotely ill at ease,' he reassured her, registering the tears that glistened in her eyes like a punch. Then, because she had her arms held in front of her chest, her hands clenched in front of her breastbone, he dropped his gaze there and said gently, 'Show me.'

Hesitantly she lowered her arms, and Fabian was confronted by the cruel scarring that violated the soft pearly skin between her breasts. Protest at the wicked desecration was arising passionately inside him, but he could not find the words to express his emotion right then.

'It was caused by a jagged piece of metal in the crash…the same as here.' She touched her hand briefly to her forehead. Clearing her throat, she formed her lips into an anxious little smile. 'I'm sorry, Fabian… I'd hardly make the kind of impression I expect you'd like in these beautiful gowns. I should have told you about this yesterday.'

'Do not blame yourself. I hardly gave you a chance, did I?'

'This does not have to be the end of the world, no?' Suddenly Dante was beside them both, his expressive face enthused with renewed purpose. 'I am not known as the maestro for nothing! I have accessories that can create magic better than any illusionist! And I have brought other less revealing gowns that will be equally stunning on the beautiful Laura, and will not make her self-conscious about these silly little scars! Life deals us all blows, *signorina*,' he said with a glint of moisture in his sable eyes. 'Some visible, some not so. But we do not have to let them destroy our ability to enjoy the beauty in life…*si*?'

Briefly meeting Fabian's concerned glance, Laura wiped at her own tears, then smiled without restraint at the other man who stood there. For a disconcerting instant Fabian sensed his heartbeat quicken at the gesture.

'You are right, Signor Pasolini. I am sorry I made a fuss,' he heard her say, and he had to seriously fight not to impel her into his arms there and then and kiss her. 'Fabian…would you mind leaving us again?'

'You are sure you want to do this?' he asked a little gruffly.

'I don't want to let you down tonight,' she replied, her soft gaze like a jewelled misty dawn.

'I know that will not happen.'

Turning away, Fabian returned to the adjoining salon and, instead of sitting, walked straight to the window and gazed out unseeingly at the busy scenes of activity in front of him. The preparations for tonight's event were underway with a vengeance, but now he anticipated it with even less enthusiasm than usual. Instead he pondered the devastating effects—both mental and physical—the car accident must have made Laura suffer, and a profound stab of unease and regret pulsed through him.

He should not have coerced her into trying on the dresses—and he would not have if he'd known why she was so reticent. Yet it struck him how dignified and beautiful she'd appeared in the stunning red dress, in spite of her scars. *She would make an ideal wife for him.* Not showy or avaricious, but composed and serene—he would be able to take her anywhere. Maybe, given time, they might even become good friends? Reluctantly recalling the husband she had lost, he refused to consider that Laura might well refuse his offer of marriage because she was afraid that this marriage too would ultimately end in disaster. She had said that marriage should involve much more than clear-headed logic! Clearly a woman of deeply held passions, could she be satisfied with the kind of loveless arrangement that Fabian was suggesting? Albeit one that had numerous attractive benefits, in his opinion?

Clenching his jaw grimly, he determinedly pushed the disquieting possibility of her refusal away.

A couple of hours before the concert—when the phones had finally stopped ringing and all the last-minute arrangements had been taken care of—Laura stretched her arms high above her head at her desk and groaned. The muscles at the back of her neck and across her shoulders cramped painfully, testimony to the tension that had been slowly building all day.

It had started with that scene earlier on, when she'd tried on the stunning red dress Dante Pasolini had brought and had known she couldn't hide her scars any longer. *She had never felt more vulnerable or scared than she had in that moment.* But the fashion designer had turned out to be the kindest of men, and when Fabian had walked in and seen the scar too the gaze that had swept over her had been anything but repulsed, as Laura had feared it might be. She had definitely seen compassion in his eyes—and how could a man who demonstrated that admirable quality so naturally profess to almost scorn love as he did? What his wife had done had obviously made him deeply cynical about trusting his heart.

Adding to Laura's discomfort now was not just the

fact that she had to present some of the performers during the evening, and act as her boss's hostess, but that after the concert she had promised Fabian to give him her final answer regarding his marriage proposal. He might want her to treat it like a business proposition, but every time she thought about it her stomach was flooded with butterflies the size of small helicopters.

'Laura…why are you still at your desk? You should have finished work at least half an hour ago! It is nearly time to get ready.'

He'd entered the room barefooted, as was his custom when he was at home, and—wrapped up in her own pressing concerns—Laura hadn't heard him.

'I was only seeing to a few last-minute things,' she said, turning. 'A couple of guests lost their invitations, and there were one or two requests from people travelling from further afield for directions to the villa.'

But Fabian hardly seemed to be listening to any of this. Instead he was frowning deeply as he regarded her. 'You look tired and drawn, and there are dark circles beneath your eyes.'

'I'll be fine when I shower and freshen up. You'd be amazed at the transformation a little make-up can effect!'

Ignoring her false attempt at humour, Fabian frowned again, and the furrow between his golden brows didn't disappear.

'No doubt you are far too tense. This morning was an ordeal for you, instead of the pleasure I intended.'

Without waiting for her to comment, he swivelled her chair around and slid his hand beneath her hair behind her neck. Gently but firmly he started to knead the muscles there. His touch was silk and velvet, summer rain and scorching sun, all rolled into one. For weak-willed moments Laura let herself bask in the almost unbearable pleasure of it. Then she abruptly brought herself to her senses and told herself she shouldn't be encouraging him to touch her like this. It was simply too intimate, and it crushed all possibility of making rational decisions where he was concerned ever again.

'You have to stop.' She laid her hand over his and pulled it away. Turning in her seat, she lifted her gaze to his in mute appeal.

'Why?'

'You ask me that when—'

'When what?'

'When you are confusing me to such a degree that I can't even remember my own name!'

Rising to her feet, she found herself with bare inches between their two bodies. He was smiling at her, and that confused her even more. With his slightly crumpled white linen shirt, softly napped jeans, bronzed skin and sun-kissed hair, he was the kind of fantasy that she'd never dreamt would come into her sphere.

'Don't, Fabian!'

'What have I done?' he asked, in apparent inno-cence.

You're leading me down a road I am frightened to go down, Laura answered in the silence of her mind. *And yet every second you smile at me the temptation to travel it grows too great to resist.*

'I'm only here to work for you, and you're treating me like—like something far more personal than that.'

'I have asked you to be my wife…remember?'

'But the marriage you have in mind is hardly a proper one.'

'It will be legal and proper in every way!' He looked affronted for a moment.

Sensing this was not the time to confront the is-sue, Laura sighed. 'You know what I mean! But I suppose we have no choice but to wait until later to discuss it properly. Well…I'd better go and get ready for the evening.'

'Before you do that I think you should get a massage first. Iron is more yielding than the muscles in the back of your neck! And I want you to be as relaxed as possible tonight, so that you will enjoy the occasion and not dread it.'

His words brought up a new concern. 'Are *you* dreading it, Fabian?' she asked quietly.

'What do you mean?'

'I haven't been immune to the fact that you seem

a little less than thrilled about the whole event…yet your dedication to helping the children at the hospice is unquestionable!'

Her comment definitely seemed to take him aback. The very blue irises around much darker pupils seemed to acquire an even more intense hue. 'You are an astute woman, and I cannot deny that promoting and holding this concert brings up some difficult challenges for me personally. But this is not something that I want to consider right now, when I am just a short time away from greeting my guests… *si*?'

'Yes, I understand.'

'Come with me.' Getting hold of her hand, he steered her firmly towards the door.

'Where are you—?'

But Fabian wouldn't say where he was taking her, and Laura had no choice but to allow him to lead her through corridors and vestibules she'd never entered before, and finally down some marble steps to an area that was done out like a Roman spa—complete with inviting swimming pool, and the scent of lemon and pine and sweet herbs clinging to the moist air.

As she glanced interestedly at the beautiful marble statues of scantily clad women that appeared to have been modelled on Botticelli's Venus, arranged at equally measured distances across an intricate mosaic-tiled floor, a door opened to the right of them and a young man stepped out. Clad in fitted white T-shirt and shorts, with bronzed skin, silky toned muscles and dark curling hair, he couldn't have been much more than twenty.

'*Ciao*, Giuseppe!' Going forward, his hand still firmly clasping Laura's, Fabian greeted the younger man with a friendly slap on his hard-muscled bicep. 'This is Laura, who has been standing in for Carmela the past few days,' he explained in English. 'She has been working extremely hard, helping to organise the concert tonight, and is in need of a massage.'

'Fabian—no!' Her expression aghast, Laura felt her limbs turn to jelly at the mere idea of this young Hercules applying his practised hands to her pale and less than perfect flesh, with its disfiguring scars. What was Fabian trying to do to her, plunging her into all these uncomfortable situations? Force her to confront the fact that she was different from every other woman he knew? She already knew that.

'She is a little shy,' he told Giuseppe with an enigmatic smile. 'Just her neck, shoulders and back will do. Can you find your own way back to your rooms?' he asked, his avid gaze latching onto Laura's again.

'But, Fabian, I—'

'You are in good hands with Giuseppe. There is no need to be anxious. He may be young, but he is a master of his craft. I will see you in about an hour and a half at the front entrance. I want you to be with me when I greet our guests. *Ciao.*'

Leaning forward, he planted a soft kiss at the side of her jaw, just beneath her ear, and Laura sensed heat rush into her with force—especially as he had done it in front of the young masseur.

'*Signorina?*' Giuseppe was holding the door open for her with a smile that was both reassuring and inviting. 'Do not worry… I will make you feel like a new woman!' he promised, and Laura felt her ensuing blush right down to the very edges of her toes.

CHAPTER SEVEN

THE young tenor's voice elicited goosebumps up and down Laura's body. Accompanied by a magical Spanish guitar, it was the ultimate gift after all her hard work over the past few days, and made every worry and doubt she'd had about the concert melt away.

Seated in the front row of the beautifully decorated marquee, with Fabian beside her dressed in matchless Italian tailoring, making her pulse-rate soar and her heart leap every time she glanced at him, she momentarily shut her eyes and let the mesmerising sound carry her away. The music seemed to enter her bloodstream—the young singer's voice, along with the heartrending words that he sang, eliciting such deep sorrow inside her that it was almost too much to bear.

Behind her closed lids her eyes were drowned in tears. She had travelled so far to be where she was now, and when she looked back it was nothing short of a miracle that she'd made it.

Before she could regain her composure, a hand covered hers and comfortingly squeezed it. Glancing round in surprise, Laura's moist gaze locked onto Fabian's, and she was startled by the apparent concern that blazed back at her. For a man who seemed to regard emotion as a necessary evil at best, and an illogical inconvenience at worst, his actions were almost incomprehensible to her. Managing the faintest of smiles, she slid her hand out from beneath his—even though she secretly longed to keep it there—and reached into her evening purse for a tissue.

All too soon the fabulous glittering concert came to an end. Fabian brought the evening to a close by thanking all the artists for donating their incredible performances, then the guests for their 'very generous and welcome contributions' to the hospice fund and finally Laura herself for her hard work and dedication in helping to organise the event in Carmela's absence—he indicated that she join him on stage and she was truly taken aback when a pretty girl dressed all in white presented her with a huge bouquet of cream roses. As she accepted the unexpected token of thanks Fabian stepped forward and, instead of the customary kiss on both cheeks, stunned her completely—and no doubt everyone in the audience too—by kissing her full on the mouth, deliberately letting his lips linger there for a very long moment.

When he broke away his gorgeous blue eyes were twinkling with almost boyish satisfaction and an undeniable hint of mischief in their hypnotic depths. Her senses already swimming with the heady scent of the roses, Laura wondered how she remained standing she was besieged by such intoxicating dizziness. Reaching for her hand, Fabian thanked everyone again and left the stage to applause that was buzzing with frank curiosity as well as appreciation of the night's events. Laura imagined they were thinking who was she to command such personal attention from their handsome host? As soon as they descended the steps, they were instantly surrounded by a veritable swarm of people, shouting questions as well as congratulations at Fabian. Catching a brief glimpse of the reserve that seemed to slot into automatic place in his otherwise amiable expression as he pressed her close into his side—Laura sensed that all he wanted to do just then was get away from the clamouring crowd and be alone for a few minutes. Knowing that wasn't going to happen any time soon judging by the melee around them, she too longed to have some private time to herself to assimilate all that had gone on...particularly Fabian's very public kiss on her lips.

Suddenly, in the midst of the clamouring throng, Aurelia Visconti appeared. The crowd parted like the Red Sea to let her through, so that the diva could reach the man whose attention they all seemed to crave, and all eyes were suddenly on her lush figure, shown off to maximum effect in a shimmering black gown with a plunging neckline. Deliberately not acknowledging Laura in any way, she curled her fingers round Fabian's arm, as if to claim him for herself, leant towards him and whispered something in his ear.

He turned back apologetically to Laura. 'I am sorry, but I am going to have to leave you alone for a little while. Do you mind? I will be back soon.' His glance was rueful, but nonetheless told Laura that whatever he was going to do couldn't be avoided. A faint swirl of his hypnotic aftershave drifted beneath her nose, and all of a sudden he'd left with Aurelia.

Seconds later the disappointed crowd reluctantly dispersed, leaving Laura standing there clutching her bouquet alone. Helplessly, *jealously*, her gaze followed the glamorous pair—clearly heading for somewhere more private. The moment the striking soprano steered Fabian out of the marquee altogether Laura felt almost faint from hurt and disappointment.

It wasn't until the majority of the concert's audience had left, and the remaining invited guests staying for supper had filed into another lavishly decorated marquee, that Laura saw Fabian again. With no sign of the possessive Aurelia—even though she was one of his guests of honour—Laura wondered what was the reason for the older woman's absence.

Glimpsing a distinct mark of scarlet lipstick at the edge of Fabian's chiselled jaw, she felt her heartbeat go wild in anguished protest. She'd nursed the ridiculous hope that maybe the two weren't as close as things indicated, but now she knew different. Clearly the two of them had slipped away to be intimate, and she had been left to talk to Fabian's guests and reassure them of his imminent return on her own.

Suddenly the magic of the wonderful evening turned to dust, like a handful of brittle autumn leaves clasped in her palm, and as Fabian gestured that she come and sit beside him at the top table her feet obeyed reluctantly. There was suddenly a great impulse in her to escape and mull over her unhappiness in private.

'You look very beautiful in that dress,' he said, his accented voice velvety pitched and intimate. But Laura didn't *feel* very beautiful. Not any more… Even though the dress Dante and she had finally chosen was a stunning creation of ice-green silk with a halter-necked front high enough to hide her scars and a back that plunged daringly low. All she could focus on was the lipstick mark left by Aurelia.

'Very sexy. You must keep it and wear it just for me,' Fabian continued, pinning her to the spot with his hot, hungry gaze.

Thinking of what he might have been doing with another woman just minutes ago, as well as the controversial business proposition that still awaited Laura's answer, she feverishly grasped at the need for some perspective on the situation before her heightened feelings careened out of control.

'You know I can't do that.'

'Why not?'

'Because it's *haute couture*, and I'm well aware that it's probably worth a small fortune!'

'What high-minded principles you have, Laura! I have never known a woman to refuse a gift of mine yet, and you are not just *any* woman! You know what I refer to.'

She did—and the thought made her swallow hard.

'It is still too much, Fabian.'

'Then you would deny me the pleasure of giving you this gift, and that does *not* make me feel good.'

Although he was still smiling, his glance had slightly chilled, and Laura wondered how she had seemingly acquired quite the talent for saying the wrong thing to him.

'I'm sorry… I didn't mean to sound so ungrateful.' Her spirits sank even further at his rebuke. 'It's an extremely kind gesture…thank you. And I didn't get a chance to thank you for the massage earlier either.'

Embarrassed heat cascaded spectacularly through her as she realised how that might sound to anyone overhearing their conversation. Though this time

Fabian was looking anything *but* chilly. Leaning even closer towards her—so close that she could feel the warmth of his breath skim across her mouth—he seemed suddenly fascinated by that particular part of her anatomy.

'Would it surprise you to know that I was jealous of Giuseppe this afternoon? So jealous that I found it extremely hard to concentrate on anything else after I left you.'

'Fabian…why isn't Aurelia here?'

Her question, used to deflect the frighteningly intimate nature of his conversation, didn't seem to particularly perturb him. Those broad shoulders of his, encased in exquisite tailoring, lifted in a nonchalant shrug. 'She suddenly found that she had another engagement to go to.'

'I wish—'

'What is it you wish, Laura?'

'I wish that you would tell me—'

'Your eyes are full of questions…but we cannot discuss them now. I am afraid it might look like I am neglecting my guests if I just talk to you alone…as much as that is my preference.'

Giving her an enigmatic smile, he turned to the glamorous middle-aged mayor's wife sitting on the other side of him, who was quite volubly announcing what a fantastic evening it had been and how she was already looking forward to the event next year.

* * *

'Alla salute!'

'What are we toasting?'

'The welcome end to a very successful evening, I think.'

As he pulled out a chair at a table for two, positioned on the terrace overlooking the olive groves, the peaceful Mediterranean night with its array of stars wrapped itself around them in a glittering dark stole. Fabian took a sip of his sambuca, savouring with pleasure the burst of warm aniseed that flooded his tastebuds. Opposite him, Laura took an experimental sip of the liqueur that was his personal favourite, and ran the tip of her tongue round her sweetly shaped top lip. A singular tightening gripped him low in his belly, and the quiet but forceful thrum of sexual need lit a match to his already heated blood.

Aurelia had done her best to entice him away to her own villa for the night, and had left in a huff when he'd refused her. But there was only one woman who interested Fabian enough right now for him to want to spend the night with, and that was the slender grey-eyed blonde, with her air of fragility yet uncommon strength too, in front of him.

'Why welcome?' she asked now, the thin stem of her liqueur glass positioned carefully between finger and thumb.

'Because...' he drawled, with a non-committal shrug. The protective wall he automatically employed when it came to his past had slammed into place. Now that the whole event was over there was a strong need in him to put it behind him and concentrate on the immediate future instead. A future in which he had certain hopes he was anxious would come to fruition.

'Because what? Why won't you talk to me about it?'

'I would much rather talk about something else. Such as the proposal I made to you. Do you have an answer for me yet?'

Not welcoming the uncertainty that gripped him suddenly, Fabian broodingly examined Laura's face, to try and ascertain whether her answer was going to be positive or negative. He strove hard to contain his own impatience. Sighing softly, she returned her glass to the table.

'Before we discuss that, I'd like to know why you seemed so on edge about the concert. You indicated before that your father was cruel… Holding these concerts on his behalf must bring back some less than happy memories for you, I'm sure?'

'Happy?' he mocked. 'That is not an adjective that I would use to describe anything remotely associated with my father! In our home, he ruled like a dictator!' The words left him with all the brute force of a fist slamming into his gut. 'No…remembering him does *not* make for happy memories, Laura! How could it? My mother and I were nothing but possessions to him…like ornaments he could move from room to room, or crush beneath his boot if he so willed!'

Tipping back his head, he drained the liqueur glass dry in one swallow. As the effect of the alcohol hit, Fabian let the still painful memories briefly resurface.

'To the outside world he was a man to admire…to *envy*. He had power, wealth, a beautiful wife and a son. But to us he was everything opposite to that. He used to show me off to his friends, praise me and build me up in their presence so that they would see how devoted he was as a parent. But when we were alone again he would beat me for letting him down! For shaming him with my ingratitude and surly looks! My mother was worn down by his cruelty and disdain, and it was no surprise to me when she became ill. She never recovered. I think she was pleased to be leaving this world in the end, and going to a place where he could not follow!'

'But surely she didn't want to leave her only child behind with such a man? Oh, Fabian! Why didn't she just leave him? Get a divorce so that the two of you could have had a better life without him?'

'That was never a possibility. My mother did not believe in divorce. Her faith dictated that she had made her bed and she should lie in it, and so she suffered in silence…' His lips twisted derisively, indicating he was a million miles away from agreeing to such useless and pointless sacrifice. 'Although I am sure she did not believe that I should suffer too, she was probably too weary to fight what she saw as an inevitable conclusion to the whole sorry scenario. Anyway…Roberto would have *killed* her before he would ever let her humiliate him by leaving him… never mind allowing her to take me with her!'

At his words, the colour seemed to drain out of Laura's face. He supposed a sensitive woman like her would be even more appalled by the brutish behaviour of a man like his father than most. Especially after what she had endured at the hands of her own bullying husband.

'I feel for you, Fabian. Your childhood must have been a particularly tough one, having to deal with such a harsh situation.'

'And that is why I intend to be a very different father to my own children. Which brings me back to the subject I would very much prefer to discuss.'

Refilling their glasses with more sambuca, Fabian was anxious to bring the topic to a swift and thankful close.

'You have gone very quiet, Laura…is anything wrong?'

'I am just sad that you suffered so as a child…I almost can't bear to think of it!'

'You have a soft heart.'

The small boy hidden away inside him leapt in gratitude and recognition at the kindness in her words. Yet he could not let her see how deeply they affected him.

'It's human to empathise with another's pain,' Laura went on, 'and if I had one wish it would be that no child in this world had to suffer! But if the harsh treatment from your father has made you vow to be a much better one…then something good can come out of it. I've learned that there are lessons in everything, and whether we like it or not adversity tempers us. All the illusions fall away, and we get to appreciate what's important in life.'

For a woman so young, she had unexpected wisdom, and Fabian couldn't help but silently affirm that when it came to choosing the perfect wife and mother of his children…he had surely made the right decision in asking Laura to fulfil that role.

'By the way,' she asked, 'why did you kiss me onstage, in front of everybody?'

'Because you looked like a rabbit caught in headlights, and I wanted to put you at ease.'

'Oh…'

'And it was also an ideal opportunity to let people know that I am personally interested in you. One more thing…'

'What?'

'You have a very sinful mouth, Laura…did you not know that?'

She blushed, as Fabian had known she would, but

composed herself quickly. 'There's something else I need to ask you.' Her bottom lip was suddenly coming under unfair treatment from her teeth. 'Are you having an affair with Aurelia Visconti?'

He laughed harshly. As attractive and talented as the demanding diva might be, he had no desire to take their relationship any further than friendship—despite Aurelia's many efforts to persuade him differently. Besides, she was far too showy and self-centred for his taste—and no doubt promiscuous too. He had already lived with a woman who was frighteningly similar. A woman who had done much more than just flirt with some of Fabian's business associates behind his back, and who had made him look like the biggest fool who ever lived! No…considering the highly desirable qualities of the serene young woman in front of him, Aurelia posed no competition for his attention whatsoever.

'No. I am not.'

'So did she really have another engagement tonight, when she didn't turn up for the supper party?'

'The truth is she wanted me to spend the night with her and I refused,' Fabian answered bluntly.

'You weren't tempted…not even for a moment? There was a lipstick mark at the side of your jaw.' Seeing her uneasiness at relating this, Fabian felt a bolt of satisfaction rocket through him, and he had the sudden realisation she might be jealous.

'Was there? The result of a very ordinary *buona-notte* between friends. That is all.'

'I know the marriage you have proposed is some-what different from the norm, Fabian…but I *definitely* could not tolerate my husband having an affair!'

'I am not an unfaithful man, and there will be no need for an affair when we start to live together, Laura. You will be quite enough woman for me, I am sure!'

'But—'

'You doubt this?' He frowned. 'Let us try a little experiment, shall we?'

He was smiling as he left his chair and went over to draw her to her feet. Feeling her tremble, he damp-ened his forefinger with some sambuca from her glass, then traced the outline of her lips with aching slowness. The soft, shocked rasp of her breath feathered over him. Moulding his hands to the shape of her hips, he felt the sensuous fabric of her gown reveal the delicate but pleasingly sexy way she was made.

Immediately aroused, Fabian nonetheless did not allow the fiery burst of passion in his blood to dictate he demonstrate his hunger in a way that might be overwhelming. Instead, he kissed the woman in his arms with the same infinite patience and attention to detail as a dedicated watercolourist touching just the tip of his brush to a delicate petal on a stem. Stroking his palms over her breasts, he secretly thrilled to feel the instantaneous hardening of their previously soft tips against his skin. For a while he simply luxuriated in the deeply sensual pleasure this gave him, not wanting the delicious sensations to end, and soon the fire that had been simmering so provocatively within ignited into full powerful flame.

Drawing Laura hard against his chest, Fabian kissed her with every bit of need, want and lust that begged for fulfilment inside him. When he finally withdrew his mouth from hers, he saw with fierce satisfaction that her stunning grey eyes were drowsy and glazed with equal voracity and need.

'I trust I have proved to you that you need not worry about other women as far as I am concerned, Laura? There is a powerful chemistry between us… *si*? A chemistry that will ensure that *you* are the one who will have all my attention once we are married!' Possessively claiming her hips, he dragged her even closer to his aching, hard body.

'Chemistry is one thing, Fabian,' she replied, with a catch in her voice, her sweet perfume driving his already impossible desire to the point where it was almost too hard to contain, 'but there is much more to a successful partnership or marriage than that.'

'I understand you have concerns…but right now, Laura, I confess I have only one thing on my mind.'

'But—'

'Touch me.'

Taking her hand, he guided it down between their

bodies to the erection behind the discreet zip fastening of his trousers, and heard her sharp intake of breath. But she didn't pull her hand away. Fabian saw her bite her lip, as if battling to deny the demanding primal need that was clearly coursing through her veins too. He smiled lazily, knowing intuitively that this was a fight she had no chance of winning.

Lowering his voice seductively, he played with a wayward tendril of her hair. 'In bed I will make *all* your worries melt away, sweet Laura, until you can think of nothing else but the pleasure we are giving each other!'

Gazing up at him with a vulnerability that suddenly arrowed straight into his temporarily unguarded heart, she softly replied, 'That's just what I'm afraid of.'

Settling his arm around her waist, Fabian drew her away from the enchanted terrace and down a network of quiet marble corridors to the cool, dimly lit enclave of his bedroom.

He'd stripped off his jacket, shirt and tie, and kicked off his shoes. His feet were bare once more, and no socks were in evidence. But Laura's enthralled gaze did not linger on Fabian's feet for long. Not when the stunning perfection of his firmly muscled chest, broad athletic shoulders and rock-hard stomach riveted her attention like some breathtaking vision suddenly appearing before her. *He was so incredibly beautiful.*

Confronted with the reality of this fact, Laura felt her apprehension at the thought of exposing her own wounded, less than perfect body to him make all her muscles clench with fear. She backed away until her legs came into contact with the huge sleigh bed with its burgundy silk sheets behind her. She gasped in surprise, and suddenly Fabian was there before her, smiling that deep slow smile into her shy eyes and making her dissolve even before he got her into bed.

He tipped up her chin. 'I only want to make you feel good… There is nothing to fear.'

It was as though he had read her mind, and a jolt of surprise flashed through her. Transfixed, she watched as he lowered his head and, moving aside some of the fabric of her dress, pressed his lips onto the raised tissue of puckered skin that was revealed. *She shook as though she would never stop.*

'*Bella,*' he murmured.

She thought her heart would overflow. Bending lower, he reached for the hem of her dress and lifted it over her head without obstruction. The brush of silk travelling over Laura's body seemed to inflame the heat that already seemed too hot to contain inside her. Her beautiful *haute couture* dress discarded, Fabian closed the gap between them and brought that incredible chest of his flush against hers. The sensation of skin against skin was like an electrical charge that made her dizzy. Everything in Laura ached to reach out and demand more.

Their intimate proximity seemed to have the same feverish effect on him. A little push and her bottom suddenly made contact with the sensual silk of the bedspread. Dropping down onto his haunches, Fabian carefully removed her shoes, unfastening their delicate emerald-green straps whilst all the while maintaining devastating eye contact with her hypnotised glance. Leaning over her where she sat, the tips of his tarnished gold hair tickling her skin, he dropped a provocative little kiss at the side of her mouth, then another one against her throat. The trembling that gripped her seemed to increase in magnitude.

Reaching for the zip of his trousers, he freed the waistband and swiftly removed them. He did the same with the ebony silk boxer shorts he wore underneath. In awe, Laura gazed at the bronzed, firmly muscled toned skin that this action revealed, her mouth stripped of all moisture when she registered the startling evidence of his desire, and how generously he had been made.

With a knowing little smile, Fabian put his hand in the centre of her chest and tipped her back completely onto the bed. Just a brief second later and he was covering her with that incredible body, pressing her deep into the sensuous fabric beneath her, taking her mouth in a kiss that demanded everything she had to give and much more besides. With the most erotic of touches he skimmed his palms seductively across the bared satin surface of her breasts, his blue eyes intensely engaged by the sight of them. Then he lifted his head to look straight into Laura's eyes.

'You are so beautiful,' he breathed.

'When you look at me that way...I *feel* it,' she replied, her heart racing. Mark had never told her she was beautiful...he'd always been too busy pointing out her inadequacies.

In another searing hard kiss Fabian's demanding mouth met hers. His breath was hot and his tongue was erotically silky. Laura thought her desire would burst at the seams if he did not give her what she ached for soon. This man—this self-contained, unashamed denouncer of love, fighting a silent war with his past—this paradoxical man with his heaven-sent looks and melting eyes who longed for children of his own but *not* a wife he could love—had released something inside her she'd almost forgotten might be there. Something pent-up and necessary that she'd long suppressed throughout her devastatingly difficult and painful marriage to Mark.

Now, as Fabian murmured in her ear and then reached for the protection he had in his trouser pocket, she watched him roll it on over his aroused sex with bated breath. Returning to her swiftly, to drag her white silk panties urgently down over her legs, he moved her silken thighs apart with his knee and pressed deep inside her—filling and scalding her with his demanding length. Her back arched at the impact, heat ripping through her like a fire bent on consuming everything in its path, and she knew she would never forget their first intimate connection if she lived to be a hundred!

Laura clutched the smooth hard biceps that bulged like iron as he thrust into her, rocking her body in the primal rhythm of this most intimate act, secretly delighting in the feminine power that she wielded over him in that moment. It made her forget that she wasn't beautiful all over, that she had scars that would be with her for the rest of her life…*both inside and out*. Fabian was murmuring seductively to her in his own passionate tongue, and although Laura did not understand everything he said, the sound and intense expression of the words made her blood sing. Willingly she surrendered to the avalanche of feelings that seemed to hold her in thrall and build inside her, and as he drove into her again and again, holding her fast against him, she was unable to stop herself from crying her pleasure out loud to the softly cloaked night.

'You cannot hold back now, my beautiful Laura.'

'Fabian…what you're doing to me!'

'Tell me…' he whispered, before he put his mouth to her breast and sucked hard. 'What am I doing?'

'You're making me… You're making me—'

She gasped as waves of honeyed heat flowed violently through her and then, as they ebbed, turned into a sweet, languorous half-dream that meant she could barely bring herself to move. But at the same time she had the notion that she had never been more awake or aware in her entire life before.

'Don't move,' Fabian ordered gruffly, before thrusting into Laura one last time and groaning his own intense satisfaction as his head fell forward between her breasts.

'I couldn't move even if I wanted to,' she whispered, her lips edging into a smile.

'Marry me,' he said, raising his head, want and need flaring bright in his eyes.

A crescendo of longing swept through Laura's heart. How could she think of refusing him when he was everything she'd ever dreamed of in a man? She might be judged weak and too reckless for words, accepting such a proposal from him, but her feelings had a life and a mind of their own, and they were far too powerful to ignore.

She thought about the small boy who'd suffered such a hurtful childhood—ill-treated by his father and losing his mother far too young—and at the same time she thought about Fabian's need to redress the balance by being a good father to a child or children of his own. And Laura thought about her *own* fierce need to be a mother.

'All right,' she heard herself say. 'I will.'

Lifting her hand, she stroked the thick tarnished gold strands of his temptingly silky hair, and he turned his lips into her palm and kissed her. Sensing her heart swell with emotion, she knew that she'd reached her decision long before he'd felt moved to ask her the question again.

CHAPTER EIGHT

'WE SHOULD go to Roma.'

'Rome?'

'*Si*—I have an apartment there. We can have a short holiday and take the opportunity to spend some time alone together. I will show you all the places and sights that the tourists like to see, and some of the not so famous ones that only the locals know about… Sound good?'

'It sounds wonderful… But, Fabian?'

'You have reservations about this idea?'

He said all this as he was dressing, and as Laura watched him button up his immaculate white shirt over that heavenly chest, with its slick, solid musculature, she felt as if she was suspended in some euphoric dream she never wanted to wake up from.

The past two weeks had been a whirl of organisation and activity, with an emotional trip back to England for Laura to spend time with her parents before returning to Tuscany and an impatient Fabian back at the Villa de Rosa. Her family had been dumbstruck she'd made such a shock decision to remarry—and to a man she 'barely knew'. She'd just about convinced them she really *did* know what she was doing, and had not finally succumbed to a breakdown after all that had happened.

The civil ceremony for Laura and Fabian's marriage had taken place just yesterday. Their two witnesses had been a supportive and excited Carmela, back from honeymoon—she believed Laura and her enigmatic boss to be genuinely in love—and Maria. The charming Cybele had been a flower girl, and afterwards just a few select friends of Fabian's had been invited to a discreetly located restaurant for the wedding supper.

But the future she faced was no romantic walk into the sunset with the man she adored. Despite his amorous attentions and apparent concern for her welfare, Fabian had not married Laura because he loved her. He had married her because he desperately wanted an heir and she was the most suitable candidate.

Now, with just a sheet to cover her, she sat on the edge of the fabulous bed in their room and tried hard to put her thoughts in order. Events had run away with her, and it was time to take a good look at exactly what she'd done. From now on she was no longer 'anonymous' Laura Greenwood, but Signora

Moritzzoni of the fabulous Villa de Rosa. Her husband was a wealthy and influential man who commanded respect in this part of the world where he came from—where a family's name and lineage was everything. Laura would bear his children, and to all intents and purposes be his partner, but she could not expect ever to receive his love or devotion in return.

Her stomach plunged at the thought. Her feelings for him made the whole idea of this marriage of convenience a farce. How long could she keep up the charade of containing them when that was clearly not what Fabian wanted or expected? After the experience she'd literally only just survived with Mark, why had she been so utterly reckless as to dance so close to the volcano's edge again? The answer was that she'd married Fabian because after the trauma of the past few years she still dared to dream that a bright future might be hers. *He wasn't anything like Mark…* She knew that. There was something special about him that was nothing to do with wealth, status, talent or even the extraordinary beauty he possessed that would stop any woman in her tracks.

And, although it grieved Laura that he had referred to the proposed trip to Rome as a 'short holiday', and not the romantic honeymoon she secretly longed for it to be, she was determined to take each day at a time and cherish that dream of hers no matter what.

'I don't have any reservations. It's just that after last night—'

'Last night was beautiful.'

With a grin that was part cat-that-got-the-cream and part unashamed seducer, Fabian was suddenly in front of her, urging her to her feet. He teasingly kissed the tip of her nose, his hypnotic azure gaze and clean masculine smell sending shivers of appreciation and want cascading through Laura's body all over again.

'We didn't get much sleep—I know that!' Trying to delicately extricate herself, when his hands were busy impelling her hips towards his, she grabbed hold of the sheet and held it fast, so that there was no danger of it slipping down.

'It was our wedding night…did you really expect to *sleep*?' he mocked gently.

'Perhaps not…but right now I need some time to relax and get my head together. I feel almost dizzy with all that's happened!'

'Well, *Signora* Moritzzoni…we will breakfast on the terrace by the orangerie, and you can take all the time you want to think about events. Yesterday went well, no?'

'Yes…it went very well.'

'And there is nothing worrying you?'

'Only that you don't regret what we've done? Getting married, I mean? What if you meet somebody you *really* fall in love with, Fabian? Have you thought of that? You might grow to resent tying yourself to me then!'

'You are such a foolish little romantic, my sweet Laura!'

Even though his words pierced her heart, Fabian's glance was unmistakably tender in that indelible moment when he cupped her face between his hands and gazed into her eyes.

'There is no possibility of any such thing happening to me. I know exactly what I am doing, and why, and I do not regret a thing! I told you before that emotions are not to be trusted, and I stand by that statement. In time I do not doubt that you and I will become good friends…we are already lovers…and when we have our children we will have a marriage based on a solid foundation of friendship and respect—not something built on a precarious little love affair that fizzled out after just a few weeks or months!'

Laura was silent, even though his disbelief in love stung worse than the sharpened points of a thousand swords digging into her flesh. Was he destined to be cynical about love for the rest of his life because of his ex-wife's behaviour? She wanted to ask him more about his past and her, but she sensed it was a topic he wouldn't readily discuss. She had brought shame on him, he had told her, and now there was a wall in him because of it…a wall that sooner or later she would have to crack if their future lives together had any chance of success at all. She made herself change the subject. 'By the way…regarding my return to work. I want to look for a post teaching music to children fairly soon. I've been away from it too long since the accident and I need to get back to doing what I love. You said you would respect my wishes about this.'

'Of course.' Moving even closer, Fabian lifted a few strands of her wheat-gold hair and just stared at them as if contemplating something profound. But then his gaze sank back into hers once again and made Laura's breath catch. 'It will not be a problem. You have my promise that you may work up until such time as you are pregnant with my child. But after that…the situation will have to be reviewed. Agreed?'

At the idea of falling pregnant with her husband's child, Laura's stomach fluttered half with joy and half with fear. Having Fabian's baby would bind her to him with love even more…how could it not? One day he would realise that she loved him and what then? Her mouth was suddenly so dry that she could barely speak her answer. 'Agreed.'

'And the perfect teaching post for you will not be hard to find. I have a lot of contacts in both the arts and in other areas of education and you will soon be doing the work you love again.'

'That would please me but…' Hectic colour swam

into Laura's cheeks at the almost 'predatory' way Fabian was suddenly regarding her and she deliberately pulled her glance from his, determined to finish what she was saying. 'I don't want any special favours. I'd like to win the right position on my own merit. Not because you used your influence in any way! Now I need to shower and dress. I've lingered here too long and I— Stop looking at me like that!'

'You seriously expect me not to be aroused when I know you are naked under that sheet? If so…you attribute to me powers of self-control I do not possess where you are concerned! After the intensity of pleasure last night, my body cannot help craving yours again! I mean it as a compliment. You are a very desirable woman with all the womanly attributes a man could want…and try as I might, I cannot resist the hot demand that burns in my blood for you!'

Before Laura could gather her wits, his lips seared hers in a kiss that completely obliterated the flimsy vestiges of her resistance as though it was nothing at all and she found herself clinging to him with an uncontained moan of longing and delight as he stripped away the sheet she wore and let it drift to the floor in a soft burgundy pool at her feet….

Rome—noisy, beautiful, vibrant—descriptions were legendary and myriad and it was one of Fabian's favourite cities in the world. He had an apartment in the Piazza Navona that overlooked the impressive fountain of Neptune. Fashionably decorated but with its fair share of faded grandeur in keeping with the building's age—it was a place that had no associations with his father whatsoever. When Fabian had left Tuscany to go to university to study art—he had gone to Rome. His first taste of freedom—it had held an affectionate place in his heart ever since. Now he wanted to show what it had to offer to Laura—the woman who was now his wife. A memory came to him as they strolled together down the narrow bustling side streets that led away from the *piazza*— a memory of tears glistening in her beautiful eyes when they had been listening to that young tenor singing. He had reached for her hand to comfort her because he'd intuited that the sorrow in her was a deep, far-reaching river and the singer's voice had merely been a catalyst to opening the floodgates of sadness that dwelled inside. He had not yet asked her properly about the accident or about the husband she had lost. Now that Laura was his wife Fabian felt even less inclined to visit both those subjects—yet he could not avoid doing so for ever. If he felt a little possessive and wanted to shut out the past for both of them so that it wouldn't intrude on the pleasure of today—he told himself it was only natural. But he really did have a great desire to get to know her better and therefore, some time soon, he would have to find out the details about what happened to her. He fully intended to be the best husband he could be in this marriage. And if there were difficulties ahead, then he honestly believed they could be overcome because already they had a profoundly sensual connection that would go a long way towards healing any rifts.

'It's just as I imagined it would be.'

'It is?'

Catching her hand and knowing a fierce pleasure in keeping it in his—Fabian smiled. In her white peasant-style cotton dress with its puffed sleeves and flared skirt, her blonde hair shining and her extraordinary eyes as excited as a child's…she was definitely *molto bello*…

'Bustling, busy and everywhere you look, something beautiful or fascinating to gaze at!'

'I cannot argue with that!' He was looking at his wife, with frank male appreciation, and she stared back at him with an expression that was both shy and surprised.

Then she smiled and hit him playfully on the arm. 'You know what I mean!'

'Yes, but we have barely even started our little tour of discovery yet! There are many amazing sights in Roma to see. First of all I want to take you to a coffee bar that does the best espresso in all of Italy! It is mostly only known to locals, but I think you will like it.'

'Well, seeing as though I've become a huge fan of

your beloved espresso in the weeks since I've been here, lead on!'

In the bustling aroma-filled coffee bar, with its array of monochrome photos of 1940s and '50s jazz musicians adorning the walls, functional unfussy wooden tables and sturdy chairs, Fabian chose seats by the window so that Laura could sit and 'watch the world go by', as she so charmingly put it.

She was like an excited child today, and her enthusiasm for being in his favourite city gave him a sense of satisfaction and pleasure that took him by surprise. He also had to keep curtailing a sudden great need to touch her and hold her, and the warmth that kept invading his insides whenever his gaze met hers he stubbornly put down to excitement and pleasure— not anything more meaningful. He had been down that road of self-deception before, with Domenica, and she had exposed him for the trusting, naïve, love-struck idiot he had been—too blinded and besotted to know that his wife was fooling around behind his back.

Swallowing down the bitter memory, Fabian nodded towards the grey-paved square outside, complete with fountain and edged by yellowed crumbling buildings with dusty and in some cases ancient shop signs.

'This place used to be a flower and fruit market, but now the sellers have dwindled to just two or three. It is now mainly used as a meeting place for locals.'

'You sound like you know it well?'

'I discovered it when I was a student here. My friends and I would often meet over an espresso here, or stand in the square and put the world to rights!'

'And what did you study?' She leant towards him a little across the table, her glance intensely interested.

Quirking a philosophical eyebrow, Fabian grinned. 'What else does one study in Rome?' he asked, teasing. 'The history of art, of course!'

'What an amazing resource you had for your research!' Laura sighed. 'It must have been wonderful!'

'It was.'

'And is this where you met your ex-wife, Fabian? In Rome?'

His chest tightened uncomfortably. 'No. I met Domenica in Tuscany. Her father was a friend of my father's.'

'Domenica? That's a beautiful name.'

'She was a beautiful girl…but unfortunately her heart was *not* so beautiful.'

'Were you——?'

'Let us talk about something else. I do not care to dwell on the past today…only on the future.' His tone was firm.

'And what about the present?' Leaning back in the straight-backed chair, Laura was reflective. 'Time goes by so quickly, and sometimes we don't realise that moments are passing us by because we're not paying attention.'

'You have clearly spent a lot of time thinking about such things, I can tell.'

'After the accident, when I was in hospital, I had nothing *but* time to reflect on what life was all about. And here in the west we take so much for granted. It seems to me there's not much point in being given the gift of life if we never even pause to reflect on what is the meaning and purpose of it.'

'Well…not everyone is as conscious or as appreciative of the gift we have been given as you, my sweet Laura. Most people behave as though they are going to be here for ever!'

'Sometimes it takes something momentous like an accident or an illness to wake people up. Don't you think it would be better if they woke up to their life *before* that point?'

'I am beginning to think that I have married a budding psychotherapist!'

'I'm sorry.' A crimson tide swept into her cheeks. 'I tend to get a little carried away when I'm talking about these things.'

'Do not apologise. Passion and enthusiasm are not things to be ashamed of.' Reaching for her hand, Fabian stroked his thumb back and forth over her flawless porcelain skin. 'I like it that you feel things so strongly.'

'Do you?' Suddenly still, her steady thoughtful gaze dived deep into his. 'I thought you believed that feelings aren't to be trusted?'

An intensely awkward few seconds ensued as Fabian fought hard to keep his treacherous feelings under control. With a self-deprecating grimace, he lifted his coffee cup in the gesture of a toast. 'You have backed me into a corner, I fear…*touché.*'

'Well…' Her hand shook a little as Laura swept her fingers through her hair, and he saw that she was embarrassed as well as a little upset.

He silently abhorred his inability to make the kind of real connection he secretly craved with her. Then, in the next second, he told himself he would get over it. His reactions were all at sea because for the first time in months he was starting to relax, as he was here in his favourite city with the pretty, vivacious woman who was going to give him the thing that he desired most…a family. He could surely be forgiven if he didn't feel quite himself?

'I can't believe we flew here in a helicopter all the way from Tuscany!' she finished.

'I would never make half the meetings I have on time here in Italy without it,' Fabian replied, grateful that the tricky moment had passed.

'It's such a different way of life you lead, compared to my own back in the UK.'

'And do you think you will grow to like it?'

'I hope so.' Some of the light seemed to go out of her mercurial eyes, and the taut muscles around his stomach clenched hard in concern.

'You seem doubtful?'

'It's going to take some adjusting to, that's all. My feet feel as if they haven't touched the ground for quite a while! And now that the dust has started to settle I find myself wondering what a man like you—a man who could probably have anything in the world that he desired—including his pick of beautiful women—sees in a woman like me?'

Her hand was touching her fringe again as she said this, and Fabian frowned. 'If the scar bothers you so much, I could arrange for you to see a very good plastic surgeon. I do not like it that you feel it diminishes you somehow.'

'I don't.' She flushed. 'Not really. I've grown to accept my imperfections as time has gone on. In a way, having them has made me stronger…as well as less focused on the more superficial aspects of life. I'm just happy to still *have* my life after what happened. No…it was you I was thinking of, Fabian. You—with your beautiful house and beautiful things. You move in the kind of circles where these things matter. How will *you* cope with having a wife who hardly conforms to the standards of beauty your friends and peers might expect?'

'First of all, it is a problem only in *your* mind,

Laura…not mine! Do you think I care what anybody else thinks? After years spent living with my father I will not be dictated to on how to live my life by anyone! And beautiful things have their place, but I do not attribute such importance to them as you may think. So let us focus on the future we have resolved to make together, and not be so concerned with the opinions of others.'

'All right. I'll try.'

'You have the strength to do anything you put your mind to. I have sensed this many times since I met you.'

'I suppose I'm a survivor…that's why.'

'You are indeed a strong woman…I admire that.'

'It's funny…but after Mark I—' She cut the thought off abruptly, and even though he hated himself for it Fabian was glad.

Sitting in his favourite café on a glorious day with his pretty new wife, and contemplating an enjoyable afternoon's sightseeing, he perhaps selfishly wanted to keep the mood as light as possible. And encouraging Laura to talk about her past would probably mean that she would then turn the tables on *him*. She had already tried by bringing up the subject of his ex-wife. Wanting to resist more pain, he stayed deliberately silent.

'Fabian?'

'What is it?'

'Are you sure you don't regret—?'

'I am perfectly satisfied that I have done absolutely the right thing in marrying you, Laura. In time, you will also come to see that. Now, drink your coffee and do not spend another moment worrying. We only have a week here in Rome before we go home again, so let us just try and relax and enjoy our time together.'

CHAPTER NINE

IT WAS only the second day of their holiday. They were strolling through a busy *piazza*, having just exited a fascinating gallery of Renaissance art. One moment Laura was walking along, then the next it was as if she was in a dream sequence, where she was running but didn't seem to be able to move fast enough.

Fabian had been talking quietly at her side, pointing out landmarks as they headed towards the great cathedral of St Peters' and she had been entranced by everything. Then there had been the sound of rubber tyres screeching on concrete, a woman's scream puncturing the air, and a child's small perplexed face in the front of a small knot of people as the out-of-control motorcycle careened towards him at speed. Her attuned senses registered everything, and in less than an instant Laura found herself racing towards the child and snatching the small body safely up into the air as the motorcycle veered off course at the last second—but not before the handlebars glanced sick-eningly against her hip.

Somebody—man or woman she didn't register right then—pulled the now crying little boy out of her arms just as Laura felt herself sink to the ground in dizzying pain. The next instant Fabian was leaning over her, a stream of frantically voiced words leaving his lips but making no impression upon its recipient, his handsome face bleached of all colour and the sheen of sweat standing out on his brow. Wanting to reassure him, Laura reached out, but just as her hand touched his shirtsleeve darkness swallowed her whole…

She blinked, and blinked again. Her mouth felt like a dried-up riverbed, and the light—clinical and harsh—made her feel as if someone was sticking needles into her eyes. She heard a small sound leave her lips, but felt strangely detached from it—as though it hadn't come from her at all.

'Laura?' A hand lay on top of hers, and she saw that it was Fabian's. When she turned her head to-wards him she saw by his expression that he'd visited a place he never wanted to visit again.

'Where am I?'

'You are in the hospital. You saved a little boy from a runaway motorcycle and you were hit your-self. Do you remember?'

'I don't feel any pain.'

'The doctor gave you a painkiller as well as a sedative. You came round more or less straight away, but then in the ambulance you became very upset and agitated. Can you not remember anything?'

The concern and fear in his eyes seemed to double, and Laura again felt the strongest impulse to reassure him. 'I'm sure it will all come back to me in time. The last thing I remember was walking towards St Peter's…then there was that horrible sound of tyres screeching.' Swallowing hard over a throat that seemed to grow more parched by the second, Laura tried to sit up.

Immediately Fabian stood up from his chair by the side of the bed and started to urge her back down against the single white pillow behind her head.

'I need a drink… I'm so dry!'

'Of course you can have a drink—but do not try and sit up so suddenly.'

The plastic tumbler of cool water tasted like nectar to Laura. A few thirsty sips and she felt her head clear a little. Enough to note that she was in a small screened-off area, with the attendant sounds of a busy casualty department audible outside it.

'You risked your own life to save that child's. It was an incredible thing to do, but perhaps incredibly foolish too. My heart has barely stopped racing since it happened!'

'I'm sorry I frightened you.'

Her voice a mere husk of its normal tone, Laura stared at his still stricken face and knew she was perilously close to the kind of tears that would not be easily subdued. She felt as if something was unraveling, and she fought hard to contain the sea of emotion that swelled inside her. Fabian didn't trust emotions, she remembered, and she wouldn't disgrace herself in front of him.

'The little boy…it's coming back to me now.' She held the side of her head and frowned. 'He wasn't hurt? And what about the girl on the motorcycle?'

'The little boy was completely unscathed, thanks to you. His parents have been in the waiting room all this time, wanting to come in and thank you for what you did. The girl suffered a broken leg, I believe, and is having treatment as we speak. It could have been much worse for her…*and* you.'

There was that look on his face again—part fear, part admonishment for being so reckless. Laura sighed, glad to hear her impulsive rescue attempt had not been in vain, but also sad that what had started out a bright, hopeful day was now inevitably marred by events.

'I'd like to go home.' She wasn't entirely sure what she meant by that…where *was* her home now? 'Please…can we just go, Fabian?'

'You have to see the doctor first. You will not be able to go anywhere until you are thoroughly checked over, and I will not be taking you anywhere until you are!'

Sinking reluctantly back down onto the pillow, Laura shut her eyes to blank out the misery that suddenly descended. Why couldn't he kiss her? Be tender? Say something kind? Because the kind of marriage she had entered into with him was *not* the kind that was born out of love on his part, she reminded herself. Now all she wanted to do was curl up tight into a little ball and try and become invisible.

He had died a thousand deaths in those surreal moments when Laura had suddenly left his side and sprinted like an athlete towards the crowd of people on the opposite side of the road. His heart in his mouth, Fabian had almost caught up to her when the motorcycle had reached her first, veered sharply to the left to avoid hitting her, and then—with sickening inevitability—glanced against her anyway.

After the child had been grabbed from her arms, she had sunk to the ground as graceful as a ballerina. For a moment Fabian had been paralysed by the shock of what had happened, then he'd been leaning over her, registering with violent regret the look of pain and puzzlement on her whitened face and cursing himself for not reacting more quickly and pushing her out of the way of danger. When she had passed out he had been half out of his mind with fear, thinking he might be going to lose her, and the relief he had experienced when she'd opened her eyes again had been off the scale. But Fabian had been even more traumatised by the scene in the ambulance.

The accident seemed to have triggered distressing memories of the car accident in which her husband had been killed, and Laura had cried out his name in anguish again and again—the sound almost cutting Fabian's heart in two. Her arms had been flailing wildly, and the attendant paramedics had literally had to hold her down to prevent her from harming herself. That was when she'd been given the sedative.

Now back in his apartment, having been advised by the doctors to rest for the next couple of days, she lay on one of the sumptuous sofas in his living room, subdued and pale, her thoughts in a place where he couldn't join her.

'Why do you not try and sleep for a while, hmm?'

Lowering his hard lean frame into the armchair opposite, he rested his elbows on his knees. If a man could age a hundred years in one day, then he had surely done just that.

'I don't want to sleep.'

'Are you hurting?' Fabian's stomach rolled in a violent somersault at the idea she might be. He glanced at his watch. 'I can give you another painkiller in about an hour. They are very strong, and we have to be careful.'

'You don't have to nursemaid me!'

There it was again…that *bitter* edge to her voice that was so unlike the woman he had come to know it unsettled him completely. Shock and trauma had obviously set in, and he would have to be patient while she recuperated and returned to her true self.

'Why do you reject my help?' he asked, completely against his better judgement. Her repudiation had definitely touched a very raw nerve.

'Because I can deal with this much better on my own! Why do you assume I need the help of *any* man? All they ever seem to do is hurt me and cause me grief!' Biting her lip in anguish, she turned her face away from him.

'You called out your ex-husband's name in the ambulance…several times.' His voice low, Fabian had to garner every bit of courage he possessed to even mention the fact. But something told him if they didn't talk about it now it would fester between them like an untended wound that would grow worse, possibly poisoning any chance of truly making their union work.

'Did I?' Still she wouldn't look at him.

'You talk of grief. Do you still miss him? *Want* him?' His voice sounded as if it rolled over gravel.

'What?'

Easing herself up against the mound of cushions at her back, Laura stared at him.

'I have never heard a woman so distraught…not since my mother, of course. But that was not because she cared about my father.' Not liking the thread of pain that wove through his words, and jealous and fearful of the road his own questioning was taking him down, Fabian pushed to his feet. 'You are clearly not over him…are you, Laura?'

'How could you believe that after I told you I def-initely *wasn't* in love with him any more?' Slowly she shook her head. 'I regret that he died the way he did—of course I do! But I don't *miss* or want him! Living with Mark was like living with a time bomb—he was a gambler, a liar and a cheat, and that was just for starters! I knew our life together was going to blow up in my face one day. He was insanely jealous and possessive, and at times I was a virtual recluse in my own home because he didn't want me seeing either family or friends without him there. My only freedom was when I was working. As for my "talent"—that didn't please him at all. Quite the reverse, in fact. He viewed it as a threat—a threat that I might one day have a ticket out of the prison I was in!'

Swallowing hard, Fabian didn't remove his gaze from her for an instant.

'The day of the accident…he picked me up from work as usual, and as soon as I got into the car I could smell that he'd been drinking. I tried to get out but he pulled away quickly, guessing my intention. I found out that he'd been gambling heavily the night before and had lost virtually everything, so he was angry and resentful and wanted someone to blame for his bad luck. That role usually fell to me.'

She tossed her head a little, as if the memory cut deep and Fabian saw the glitter of tears in her eyes.

'I'd been building up to telling him I was leaving him for months before, and suddenly I couldn't hold back the words—even though I knew he'd ultimately make me pay for them. He lashed out at me, taking his hands off the steering wheel. He yelled that if I tried to leave him he would kill us both! It was a rainy evening and the tyres skidded badly on the wet road, sending the car completely off course. Drinking always brought out his darker side…especially whisky…and that was what I'd smelled on his breath. Anyway…his reactions were severely slowed down by the amount of alcohol in his blood, and before he could steer us out of the way we hit a van coming in the other direction. In the second before it happened I can remember screaming his name…I guess what happened to me today must have temporarily taken me back there. Oh, God—it was a living nightmare!'

It was then that Fabian recalled the horrified look on her face when he'd told her what his father would surely have done if his mother had sought to leave him. Laura had actually *been* in that frightening situation herself. This time he didn't resist the impulse to go to her and offer comfort. Truth to tell, he needed to be close to her right then. He could hardly believe what he had just heard, and it disturbed him deeply.

Sitting on the edge of the couch, he tipped up her chin and looked straight into her eyes. 'But that dreadful time is over now…in the past. And now you can make a new life…a much better life for yourself…free from fear and in a place where there are no difficult associations or reminders of what happened before. As soon as we return to Tuscany I will see what I can do about that teaching post. At least I can get you an interview, and the rest will be up to you.

'Your ex-husband sounds like a very dangerous man… He had the kind of problems that would inevitably have got worse over the years, and he would have made anyone close to him suffer. I cannot admit to being sorry that he is dead. Selfishly…I am glad. You carry wounds that might take a long time to properly heal, Laura, but I can help you. I will take care of you and make sure you do not come to harm. But you have to promise me not to put yourself in the way of danger again at the slightest provocation! I did not realise I was contemplating marriage with Superwoman!'

'Believe me, I'm no heroine!' Grimacing at first, her expression gradually turned into the most cautious of smiles. 'As for today, I just acted on instinct. It was because he was a child…a little boy with his whole life ahead of him. I couldn't have borne seeing him hurt, and his parents suffering for the rest of their lives!'

'Not many people would have done what you did. Again you sell yourself short. Now you must rest and recover, so that hopefully in a couple of days' time I can show you all the sights you missed seeing today!'

'Perhaps I will try and sleep a bit, then.'

Laying her head back against the bank of pillows, she let Fabian arrange the blanket more securely around her. A muscle flinched in the side of his jaw. 'Your hip will be covered in bruises tomorrow, so the doctors tell me.'

'I can believe that! I feel like I've had an argument with a battering ram!'

'It is hardly a matter to joke about!'

'Bruises will heal, Fabian…you mustn't upset yourself.'

'I just wish you had more respect for your own safety!'

'I promise no more heroics for the rest of our holiday.'

'I am going to hold you to that…you can count on it! Now, get some sleep. I will be right here if you need me.'

Laura sucked in a deeply shocked breath at the sight of the vivid bruising discolouring her hip the next morning. The mass of contusion resembled an illustrated map of the world, and would probably take a little while to fade completely. She'd slept like a baby, though, in spite of all the drama, and had woken to a sun-filled room in the huge king-sized bed that only she occupied. *But she hadn't spent the night alone.*

Fabian had joined her soon after insisting she go to bed and get a proper night's rest, and she had registered his arms around her practically the whole time. It made her feel a little fluttery inside to realise he had held her without wanting to make love—clearly solicitous of what had happened to her and not succumbing to needs of a more intimate nature. Needs that had the power to drive them into each other's arms at the slightest provocation, it seemed to Laura. And all this care and concern from a man who prided himself on staying emotionally detached...

Frowning into the bathroom mirror, her drained, tired-looking face made her stomach turn over. What now? she asked herself. Where do we go from here? Because she didn't know the answer, she turned abruptly away.

'Who is this stunning woman?'

Lifting the framed photograph off of the polished bureau, Laura studied the vivacious brunette dressed to the nines for an evening out, and concluded she didn't look unlike some glamorous sixties movie star.

'That is my mother—Eufemia.'

When Fabian didn't elaborate, just continued to study the newspaper in front of him, Laura felt her stomach plummet a little. She'd noticed that there weren't many photographs in the beautifully appointed apartment, and although she had learned some things about his less than happy family life it still surprised her. He was such a closed book, and she yearned to know more about him—about the past that had shaped him and made him an island she couldn't quite reach.

'Won't you tell me something about her?' she asked, her heart pumping slightly against her ribs.

The newspaper was lowered reluctantly, and his brows were furrowed as he turned from his seat on the couch to regard her. 'What would you like to know?'

Holding onto the photograph in its elegant frame, Laura's fingers curled round it with sudden determination.

'What kind of woman was she? Were you close to her?'

'She was both kind and sensitive—perhaps too much so—devoted to her faith and to me, her son. But she was not a strong woman like you. Hurt—however slight—could shatter her into a million pieces. It was a miracle that she survived as long as she did, married to my father. When she contracted pneumonia after a bout of flu I knew then—even though I was only ten—that it was just a matter of time before she died.'

'How sad for both of you to lose each other so early on!' Laura could only try to imagine what it must have been like for a small child of just ten to lose the mother who adored him at such a tender age, and be left alone with a father who was tyrannical and frightening. 'I can tell by the way you speak about her that you must have loved her very much.'

'Was there anything else you wanted to know?'

Even though he'd forced himself to ask the question, Laura could tell by Fabian's tone that he did not intend to easily give up any more personal information. Somehow, that made her angry, as well as regretful.

'Please don't shut me out, Fabian. I know you don't trust emotions and think they can only be misleading—but I *want* to get to know you better. Talking about the past can be painful, I know…but it can be healing too. I heard something once—after Mark—and it helped me tremendously. It was something about fear stopping you from loving…but if you let yourself love it can stop the fear. Can't you try and let down your guard a little for me? I promise never to manipulate what you tell me or use it against you in any way.'

CHAPTER TEN

ALL morning he had surreptitiously watched her, knowing by the slight limp she had acquired that she must be in pain, but was clearly putting a brave face on it for his sake. Now Fabian felt like the target for a hundred tiny but lethal arrows, aimed at unravelling the very emotions he had always scorned so disparagingly and readily—convincing himself that he was completely immune to feeling anything deeper than desire and perhaps on occasion friendship for a woman. Now Laura was making a liar of that belief, and he was having a hard job of stemming the forceful tide of feeling that was mounting inside him.

Leaving his seat, he crossed the room to where she was standing. Carefully extracting the photograph from her, he put it back in its spot on the bureau. Seeing his mother's beautiful face at close quarters again, and remembering how much he had suffered

when he'd lost her, Fabian once again retreated behind that iron defence he'd grown so familiar with.

'You are getting overwrought and that is not good
for you—especially after what happened yesterday.'
He touched her cool pale cheek with his knuckles and
saw her wince, as though his touch suddenly dis-
pleased her. A bolt of unease shuddered through him.

'Overwrought?' Her grey eyes flashed. 'Just because
I ask you to be human for a change and not this—this
impervious *rock* you're so at pains to portray!'

'What?'

'You're not made of *steel*, Fabian! You're flesh
and blood and bone, just like the rest of us!'

'What is all this about, Laura?' Catching her by a
wrist that felt fragile as glass beneath his much larger
hand, Fabian felt his temper ignite. Her words had
hit too close to home and he didn't like it. 'You seem
to be intent on demanding something that wasn't
part of our arrangement. Why is that?'

'Do you really want to know?' She tugged her
wrist out of his grasp and held it in front of her.

'*Si*…I want to know!'

'I don't think you do! I think you wish I'd just
keep quiet—rest up until I'm back to normal again
and ready to go along with whatever is good for *you*!
But you know what, Fabian? I'm not going to do that.
I'm not going to do that because I can't pretend about
my feelings, and I don't want to act as if they're not

there! Coming close to death makes you realise that it's important not to waste a single day hiding behind some hurt that's made you fear to really live! It teaches you that the only really important thing—the thing that makes this short stay on earth we all have make any sense—is *love*! That and being true to yourself, no matter what!'

'You talk of love…but love is the greatest deceiver and betrayer of all!'

'I don't agree with you. I *can't* agree with you!'

'That is your prerogative.'

'What happened to you, Fabian? I know you had a tough time growing up, and that your ex-wife cheated on you, but does that mean you have to turn your back on the possibility of love in your life for ever?'

Now the arrows had turned into fully-fledged knives…

'This discussion is pointless! We made an agreement! I set out the terms of our marriage clearly enough, didn't I? Now you are making things impossible!'

'Why?' Her gaze was anguished. 'Because I might have developed feelings for you?'

'The incident yesterday has understandably unsettled you. It has left you feeling vulnerable, perhaps even a little afraid of the future, and you are mistaking needing reassurance and a demonstration of concern for love!'

He strode away from her, frustration and fear

locking every muscle and sinew in his body tight with the most excruciating tension. He turned back to observe her, his heart constricting at the sight of the sadness and disappointment reflected on her lovely face. *But fear of being betrayed again by a woman he loved bit too deep for him to easily transcend it.* He had been so humiliated... If he didn't yield his heart then such a soul-shattering experience could never happen to him again.

'If only you would give yourself the proper time to rest and take stock, you would realise that keeping unreliable emotions out of our association is really for the best.'

'Unreliable emotions? For goodness' sake, Fabian—listen to yourself! I saw you with those children at the hospice, remember? At times you were very close to tears! Are you telling me what you felt then—what *moved* you to such depth of feeling—wasn't love? You are fooling yourself if you think you're not capable of feeling such an emotion!'

Wrapping her arms around herself, she turned away from him, clearly distraught.

What had he done? Almost as if a bolt of lightning had struck him, Fabian had a shocked awakening. In that moment he realised the kind of marriage he had trapped Laura into. She was a woman who was made for a warm, loving relationship—and he had asked her to bear his children and not engage her emotions with their father! He could hardly believe his own arogance. She was nothing like the faithless Domenica. Laura was the kind of woman a man would walk across hot coals to be with, because true beauty and compassion like hers did not come along every day! Yet could he trust his heart to the possibility that she would keep her word and stay with him? Could he believe that her feelings for him would *not* fade away in time, resulting in her being with him only out of duty and responsibility and *not* love?

Needing to gain some perspective on his racing thoughts, he walked to the door almost before he knew what he was doing and opened it wide. 'I am sorry I have caused you such distress…please believe me when I say this. It grieves me to have brought you pain in any way. I think you will be better able to calm down if I am not here for a while. I do not intend to be away long, and when I return I promise we will talk,' he told her, speaking to her back, because she did not turn round to face him.

'Fine,' she said listlessly.

He went through the door and shut it behind him.

'*Buongiorno, signora…* I'm looking for a room.' At the definitely blank expression on the elderly receptionist's face, Laura forced herself to make the Italian translation. '*Stanza libere?*'

'*Sì…sì. Per quante notti?*'

'How many nights?' She frowned, wishing her legs didn't feel so frighteningly shaky. 'Just one... *solo per una notte...grazie.*'

In the small, scrupulously clean hotel room, with its yellowed shutters and old-fashioned furniture, Laura laid out her toiletries in the tiny bathroom and washed her face. Almost on automatic pilot she put on a light application of make-up and brushed her hair.

'There,' she said out loud to the mirror, as if to bolster her courage. 'At least now I'm not in danger of making anybody believe they've seen a ghost!'

Fighting back the tears, she went back out into the small bedroom and, opening the shutters wide, gazed out at the tiny narrow street below. One day...she would stay in Rome—one more day to visit some of the sights she still wanted to see—then hopefully she'd catch a flight home tomorrow.

By now Fabian would have found the note she'd left, and would probably have resigned himself to returning to Tuscany alone. What reason would he have to remain in Rome now that Laura had effectively told him what she felt? He must know now that she couldn't fulfil his hope that she would go along with this loveless arrangement indefinitely. He'd promised that on his return to the apartment that they would talk, but so far Fabian had managed to avoid talking about the most important thing of all...his *feelings.* Laura could not believe he was as detached from her as he made out—not after the passionate nights they had shared before *and* after their marriage. But there was nothing he'd said or done that led her to think he might give in and really open up to her at last.

How could she live with him, loving him the way she did, when he was not willing to even try and knock down some of those barriers of his and openly, wholeheartedly, love her back? It had grieved her to leave, but she'd finally sensed how hopeless it all was. He had no doubt already come to the same conclusion.

'Stubborn, stubborn man!' Shaking her head in despair, she stepped back from the window and grabbed her straw bag off the tidily made bed.

Out again in the glaring Italian sunshine, she determinedly ignored the throbbing bruise on her hip and, studying the little guidebook she'd purchased from the elderly lady on Reception, headed for the Vatican and the stunning, renowned Sistine Chapel.

He had received a great shock, returning to the apartment to find Laura gone. At first when he'd realised she wasn't there Fabian had told himself she had merely gone out for some fresh air, just as he had done. But then he'd discovered the note propped up against his mother's photograph, and he had almost broken out into a sweat as he'd unfolded it to read.

Fabian

I have deceived you. I thought I could go through with this marriage of ours and keep my feelings for you under restraint, but now I know to do so would mean living the most terrible lie. I can't do that. I don't want to do that! Most of all, I know I deserve to be with someone who is not afraid or ashamed to express his feelings for me. So, despite my promise to you, I have no choice but to leave and go back to England. I do not mean to cause you pain at making this decision, but I have to be true to myself. I never meant to fall for you, but I really couldn't help it. These things are unexplainable, and I'm sure you will therefore believe unreliable.

You are a good man. I know that. And I hope that one day you really will allow yourself to fall in love with someone and have that love returned to you tenfold. I've left only a few things behind at the Villa de Rosa, and I'm sure if I ask her Carmela will forward them on to me in the UK.

I had a lovely time working with you on the concert, and I wish you everything good in life—now and always. When you are ready to think about divorce, you can get in touch with me at the address at the end of this page.

All my love,

Laura.

Fury and disbelief eating him up, Fabian screwed the note into a ball and cast it angrily aside. *How could she do this to him?* She had not even given him a chance to redeem himself! Surely he deserved better treatment than that? But, as much as he could easily descend into blaming Laura for living up his secret expectation that all the women he cared for eventually ended up leaving him one way or another, he knew it was time to take a good look at his own behaviour.

As he stood there, with the fierce afternoon sun streaming through the windows, the bright rays were like a metaphor—shining light into all the dark places inside him. Exposed—there was no longer anywhere to hide—and the truth he'd already started to intuit hit him doubly hard.

All this time he had deluded himself that he was incapable of loving a woman, and he had been wrong...so wrong. Everything Laura had accused him of was right. He *wasn't* made of steel, even if he'd tried so hard to perpetuate the lie that he was, and he did not want to spend the rest of his life in emotional isolation.

Now that he had openly admitted to himself that he was as human and fragile as anyone else, his greatest desire was to share the astonishing revelation with his wife and ask her forgiveness. But first of all he had to find her. Where would she go in a city she didn't know? She had been hurt—not just physically, but emotionally too—she would hardly be thinking straight. He hated the idea that that would make her vulnerable to possible danger.

His gut clenched and then released as he strode determinedly out through the door. He would find her…he *had* to! He would scour the whole of Rome if need be, and in the meantime he would ring the airport to check she hadn't booked the next available flight home.

The concrete steps were baking beneath the thin expensive cotton of his chinos, but Fabian ignored the fact as he sat down, staring hard at the teeming throng of people milling round the Vatican. He must have examined every face, every figure that was there, registering every colour, age and feature known to man—except the sight of the face that he longed to see the most.

Determinedly quashing the glaring possibility that he didn't have a hope of finding Laura in such a crowd, he took a moment to gather himself, and as he looked up his gaze collided with a young pretty brunette in shorts and T-shirt who had stopped in front of him, rucksack on her back, smiling at him as though she'd found the answer to her prayers. Feeling nothing but impatience at her interest, Fabian started to rise to his feet again, but found himself staying put when she stuck a map under his nose and asked him for directions.

By the time he'd described to the young tourist the route she had to take to her destination his impatience and frustration had grown tenfold. Barely acknowledging her sweetly voiced *grazie*, he pushed through more milling people with renewed purpose, his chest tightening at every glimpse of blonde or fair hair on a woman—hope soaring only to be cruelly crushed again when he realised it was not Laura. Finally moving away from the heaving mass of humanity all around him, he had a great need to breathe some freer air.

It was then that he saw her. Sitting on a low step amid a sea of strangers, she was staring down at what looked like a leaflet, her bright halo of hair reflecting the sunlight like some kind of gilded jewel. She should be wearing a hat, Fabian thought, tension and concern rippling through him. Her skin was so fair and delicate she would be susceptible to burning. In fact she shouldn't be out in the sun at all. She should be home with *him*…where she belonged…

'Have you been inside yet?' he asked as he reached her, his heart all but slamming against his ribcage at the wonderful sight of her.

She stared up at him as if in the throes of a dream. 'No…' Her voice sounded husky and deeply emotional.

'Michelangelo devoted his life to painting the frescoes on the ceiling. They say he veered between ecstatic joy and the most unbearable torment as he lived out his days doing this work. I too have known both those states since I met you, Laura.'

Dropping down beside her, his hands linked together, Fabian fought hard against the powerful need to touch her.

'I wouldn't worry about either of those conditions, Fabian.' Her gaze was briefly hard as she considered him. 'After all…they're only transient states, and they hardly mean anything—do they?'

Fielding the pain of her words, he nodded slowly. 'I suppose I deserved that. Where did you go?' he asked. 'I have been looking for you everywhere.'

'I booked myself into a small hotel. I thought I should make the most of being in the Eternal City and try and see some of the sights before I go home tomorrow.'

'You have booked a flight?'

'Not yet…but I will.'

Folding the pamphlet she'd been studying, she slipped it into the straw bag beside her on the steps.

'I would like you to come back with me to the apartment so that we can talk together properly.'

'I don't think so, Fabian. Talking—at least about things that matter—isn't really your forte, is it? You must have read my note. We both want very different things in life, so what's the point?'

He sensed a muscle flinch in the side of his cheek. 'You asked me if I intended to let what happened to me growing up and in my first marriage make me turn my back on the possibility of love for ever? My honest answer is *no*…I do not want to go through the rest of my life without love,' he said quietly, seeing her pupils darken in surprise. 'But losing the mother I adored left a gaping hole inside me that I never thought to be filled again. I believe I learned then that loving someone too much brings only pain.

'Then, when I was twenty-four, I experienced the same traumatic lesson all over again, when I fell in love for the first time. Domenica was the daughter of one of my father's wealthiest friends. Naturally, they were both eager for the match. Any opportunity for my father to extend his little empire was only to be encouraged.' He swallowed down the brief flare of resentment and continued. 'So…we married. She was nineteen years old, beautiful, and intimately aware of the power of her charms with the opposite sex. So much so that she could not help but flirt with every man who came anywhere near her! No matter how many times I told her I did not like it she refused to change her behaviour.'

Grimacing, he determinedly pressed on. 'One day I returned from a trip to the south on business, and found her in bed with one of my associates. Apart from my shock and hurt, the humiliation I felt was akin to the same sickening feeling I had experienced when my father used to put me down and make me feel so small. A part of me seemed to die that day, and my hopes for a family of my own and a happy future were completely shattered. The most distressing part was that we had only been talking about trying for a baby a few nights before I found her with her lover, but I realised her enthusiasm for becoming a mother was a complete *lie*.

'Domenica was quite an accomplished little actress. I knew that all the tears and pleas for forgiveness she bombarded me with afterwards were fake. She did not possess a remorseful bone in her body! Her only regret was that she had been found out! I also made the discovery that my business associate had not been the only infidelity since our marriage. Her deceit wounded me to the core as well as sickened me. After she left, and I divorced her, I swore I would only ever have one use for women, and in future I would definitely guard against trusting my heart where they were concerned.'

'Well…that explains a lot. But that doesn't mean that anyone you grow to love would naturally end up deceiving or leaving you, Fabian! Love is a big risk, yes…but surely it is better to risk loving someone than to let your heart atrophy from self-neglect until you die?'

The pink tip of her tongue came out and moistened her lips. Fabian scarcely knew how he didn't devour her mouth right there and then. His longing to taste and touch her was so great it was like a raging fever, stampeding through his blood.

'Your words make sense, but I was not ready to heed them until now.'

'You're not alone in not heeding advice, Fabian. When my family took an instant dislike to Mark and warned me against continuing our relationship I totally ignored them! Even though they'd done nothing but act in my best interests all my life! They could see the kind of man he was and I couldn't. Actually… that's not strictly true. I knew he had problems right from the start, but I fooled myself that if I loved him enough, and he loved me, we could sort them out together. I've only told you that so you will know I'm no expert on relationships either. I got it so badly wrong that it almost cost me my life!'

'But you learned from the experience. You did not let it poison you or harden your heart as many would have done in your position.'

Registering the relief in her eyes that he understood, Fabian smiled and then frowned.

'And, by the way, why are you not wearing a hat? This sun is far too ferocious for your fair colouring. Will you come back with me now, Laura? Apart from the fact that you need to rest after the trauma of yesterday, maybe you will find that there are—after all— more things for us to talk about than you realise?'

CHAPTER ELEVEN

AFTER the unforgiving heat outside, the air inside the apartment was blissfully cool. Removing her sandals and leaving them by the door, Laura straightened to find Fabian studying her with a look of almost burning intensity. Nothing else existed in the world for her in those breathless few moments, save for that sublime unforgettable glance on his extraordinary face.

The air grew thicker, every molecule prickling with the sheer force of his presence, laced with the kind of tension that pre-empted something cataclysmic. He too had dispensed with his footwear, and from the top of his golden head to the tips of his very sexy bare feet—everything about him elicited a physicality and sensuality that even a will of iron would have had no defences against. And right now Laura had no such dubious will at her disposal.

Her body had been trembling hard from the moment she'd glanced up from the steps outside the

Vatican and seen him standing there—like some startlingly beautiful angel just delivered to her from heaven. Her whole body ached with loving him. She hadn't made even the slightest attempt to go into the Sistine Chapel, because she'd spent the whole time staring blindly at her tourist brochure—letting it act as a shield against the hotly welling tears in her eyes every time she thought of Fabian and the fact that she was leaving, probably never to see him again.

It touched her unbearably that he'd opened his heart to her at last and told her about his painful past. It made her love and want him even more. And now it seemed her store of words had run dry, because all she could think about was the wanting…

'You are not in pain?' he asked, that arresting, accented voice of his sensually gruff.

'In pain?' Laura stared, feeling as though she was being helplessly sucked into a mesmerising sea of iridescent blue, unmatched anywhere else on earth.

'Your bruises…from yesterday?'

'I'm okay.'

'Let me see.'

'Honestly, I—'

'I want to see,' he insisted, and closed the space between them with agonising slowness.

Momentarily shutting her eyes, Laura let the provocative scent of his musky cologne seep into her own heated skin. *It was too much. He was too much...* When she opened them again, Fabian had his palm spread out over the skirt of her dress and was sliding it up her thigh. When the hem reached the area of her hipbone he moved it even further up, and tugged the side of her panties downwards so that her collection of vivid bruises was clearly visible to his intensely examining gaze. She heard the sound of his deeply indrawn breath.

'It's all right... It looks worse than it actually feels.' She attempted a smile, but it melted away like ice cream in the sun almost immediately.

'It is not all right that you got hurt again, Laura.' His glance clung passionately to hers for a few moments, before he spread his palm out across the flat plane of her stomach and slowly but deliberately directed his fingers downwards. 'In future, I will do everything in my power to stop you being hurt...that is a promise.'

Registering the words 'in future' with a leap of joy inside her chest, Laura soon had other things to focus her mind on as Fabian slid his fingers inside her pretty lace panties and into the moist heat between her thighs. Her back came into hard contact with the door with a soft thud as her lips issued a deep moan of sublime relief that seemed to emanate from the very core of her being.

Even as she made the sound Fabian moved in closer, his fingers exploring even deeper. Mindless with need and starving for his kiss, Laura put her hand behind his golden head and all but dragged his mouth down to hers. The blistering contact was like an explosion of primal need that knew no bounds. His velvet tongue scorched her, sweeping as it did into all the soft centres of her mouth, ruthlessly possessive and deluging her senses with his vital masculine taste, turning her into a complete addict for his touch.

In the meantime, his hot exploration lower down her body was producing the most unimaginable sensual tension. She felt like a high wire, strung out between two points as tight as it could possibly go. He kissed her neck and she experienced the sharp sting of his teeth in her tender flesh just as her pleasure crested and made her sigh in the most exquisite relief and joy.

'I vow to you that this is the kind of pleasure I will give to you every day from now on.' His smile was lazy, and sure, and so unbelievably sensual that just the mere sight of it could scorch the ground where they stood, Laura was certain.

'My God, Fabian! If you keep such a promise I won't be fit for anything else!'

'Then I will be fulfilling my duty as a husband to keep my gorgeous wife sated and happy, no? You must know by now that you drive me completely crazy!'

Now he rained kisses all over her face, and his hands were cupping her breasts, his thumbs moving back and forth over their tightening aching tips beneath her dress, stoking the desire that Laura knew would always be just a scant breath away when they were together.

Just as his mouth descended towards hers, Laura knew there was something she had to say…something that really *couldn't* wait.

'Fabian…' she breathed, her hands anchoring themselves on the broad slopes of the heavenly muscular shoulders beneath his shirt. 'I wanted to—you know that I'm madly in love with you, don't you?'

'But of course!' His beautiful blue eyes sparkled with mirth, and the kind of warmth Laura had dreamed of seeing there. 'It is only right when I too am crazy in love with you, *il mio l'amore*.'

'You are?'

'*Si*…and I want you to know that the love you feel for me I return to you a thousand times over! What I felt for Domenica was nothing…nothing compared to the incredible happiness and joy I feel whenever I am with you!'

'Is that the truth, Fabian?'

'I swear it!'

'Well, then…now you must kiss me before I *die* from wanting you too much!'

Slipping his hands beneath the thin straps of her summer dress, Fabian pulled them down over her breasts. In the next instant he'd removed her bra completely, and instead of her lips it was the tip of each rosy breast he was attending to with his deliciously expert tongue, and Laura tipped her head back to give him even more unrestricted access.

With a harsh-voiced moan he impelled her hard against him, pulled off her lace panties, then stripped his own clothing before anchoring his hands beneath her bottom and lifting her up so that he could plunge himself into her in one hot, sure thrust.

For one dazzling moment Laura really thought she had lost her mind. Her love and joy almost made her delirious. Being with Fabian like this, feeling the intense wellspring of love she had for him grow stronger with every passing moment, was like a miracle after what had happened with Mark. But it was also confirmation that she had been right to trust that she might love again one day, and that that love would be truly and absolutely reciprocated…

His overwhelming desire for Laura caused the heat inside Fabian to become an unstoppable inferno. Her scent was all over him, the fine perspiration that glistened on her beautiful body melding with his own, and it was as if they were two parts of a double shell that had been forced apart and now—at last—were finally brought together again. *They fitted perfectly.*

Being with Laura did not just make the hurt inside him ease, it lifted Fabian up out of the underlying anxiety and despair he'd probably known all his life since his mother died. Now he was free to love a woman as she deserved to be loved—without fear of loss or betrayal dogging his every step—and he would embrace the prospect with gratitude and contentment for the rest of his days.

Moments later, as he spilled deep inside his wife's body, he let free a cry that seemed to arise from the very centre of his soul. And in that unbelievable, magical instant he knew with a deep inner certainty that the child he longed for would be conceived soon.

Ten and a half months later...

Returning from his business trip to Milan, Fabian suddenly came to a stop outside the private suite of rooms that he shared with his wife. Filling the air was the sound of her exquisitely beautiful voice, singing. Knowing she only sang like that when she was happy, he couldn't help but smile. As he listened, every note elicited a shiver of pleasure and pride right through him, and even though he had only been absent for a single day and night he ached to see her and hold her again.

Opening the door, Fabian almost caught his breath at the heavenly sight that met his eager eyes. The spring sunshine poured its sublime bounty into the breathtaking Palladian room, lighting up every corner, and in the centre Laura was seated in a huge armchair, singing to their twin baby sons.

That was another reason he was so reluctant to

spend any time away from home these days. Just over six weeks ago Laura had given birth to his children—Enrico and Roberto—named after his father in a new spirit of real forgiveness for the wounds of the past.

His wife had taught him a valuable lesson…it was the *forgiver* who received the most benefit from the act of forgiveness. She was right. Now that Fabian no longer had the weight of all his past hurt dragging him down, he experienced a lightness of being that he had never encountered before. And he had unashamedly cried like a baby himself at his children's birth, his heart overflowing with the kind of happiness that most people could only dream of.

Now, as he entered the room and the final notes of her song floated away on the warm air, Fabian's footsteps quickened as he went towards his wife.

'Fabian!'

Her smile bewitched him, as it always did, with its ravishing innocent beauty, and he sensed the power of it piercing him deeply. Bending down, he captured her lips with his usual helpless urgency, loving the scent of sunshine and babies that she exuded, thinking it had to be the most heavenly scent on earth.

'I didn't expect you back until this afternoon!'

'I thought I would surprise you by returning earlier.'

Kneeling at her feet, he bent his head to inspect the two sleeping infants who nestled in the crook of each of her arms. 'Everything has been all right?' he asked, unable to contain the leap of concern he always felt around his family.

'Everything is fine, my darling! You mustn't worry so. The boys are healthy and well, and yesterday, when the midwife came for the last time, she said they were thriving beautifully! Relax, Fabian, and just enjoy your sons without thinking something untoward is going to happen to them!'

'I cannot help it,' he admitted, with an almost melancholic half-smile. 'I sometimes cannot believe I have been blessed with so much happiness. I fear that I will wake up one morning and find it has all been a dream!'

'It is no dream, my love.' Her voice softly reassuring, Laura passed one of the children into his arms. 'Hold Enrico for a while, and feel how real your son is! We are all here to stay, Fabian…I promise you that.'

Sighing with deep pride and contentment as he held his small son, Fabian knew his eyes poured out all the love he felt inside as he lifted his head to look at his wife.

'I love coming home to you, my sweet Laura… because I know whenever I come home heaven is waiting here for me.'

A sumptuous and seductive Regency novel

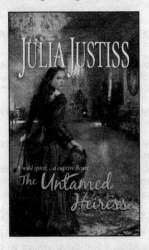

JULIA JUSTISS

A wild spirit...a captive heart.

The *Untamed* Heiress

Despite being imprisoned as a child by her spiteful father, Helena Lambarth journeys to London to enter society – and becomes a reluctant houseguest of the dashing Lord Darnell.

Saddled with his father's debts, Adam, Lord Darnell, must win the hand of wealthy Priscilla Standish. If only she weren't so ordinary compared to the unconventional Helena – who has transformed into a bewitching young woman…

Available 15th August 2008

M&B

Possessed by a passionate sheikh

The Sheikh's Bartered Bride by Lucy **Monroe**

After a whirlwind courtship, Sheikh Hakim bin
Omar al Kadar proposes marriage to shy
Catherine Benning. After their wedding day,
they travel to his desert kingdom, where
Catherine discovers that Hakim has bought her!

Sheikh's Honour by Alexandra **Sellers**

Prince and heir Sheikh Jalal was claiming all that
was his: land, title, throne…and a queen. Though
temptress Clio Blake fought against the bandit
prince's wooing like a tigress, Jalal would not be
denied his woman!

Available 19th September 2008

www.millsandboon.co.uk

M&B

4 Books
and a surprise gift!

We would like to take this opportunity to thank you for reading this Mills & Boon® book by offering you the chance to take FOUR more specially selected titles from the Modern™ series absolutely FREE! We're also making this offer to introduce you to the benefits of the Mills & Boon® Book Club—

- ★ **FREE home delivery**
- ★ **FREE gifts and competitions**
- ★ **FREE monthly Newsletter**
- ★ **Exclusive Mills & Boon Book Club offers**
- ★ **Books available before they're in the shops**

Accepting these FREE books and gift places you under no obligation to buy, you may cancel at any time, even after receiving your free shipment. Simply complete your details below and return the entire page to the address below. You don't even need a stamp!

YES! Please send me 4 free Modern books and a surprise gift. I understand that unless you hear from me, I will receive 6 superb new titles every month for just £2.99 each, postage and packing free. I am under no obligation to purchase any books and may cancel my subscription at any time. The free books and gift will be mine to keep in any case.

P8ZEF

Ms/Mrs/Miss/Mr ....Initials ....
BLOCK CAPITALS PLEASE

Surname ....

Address ....

....

....Postcode ....

Send this whole page to:
UK: FREEPOST CN81, Croydon, CR9 3WZ